ETHAN

BETWEEN

US

ALSO BY ANNA MYERS

RED-DIRT JESSIE

ROSIE'S TIGER

GRAVEYARD GIRL

FIRE IN THE HILLS

SPOTTING THE LEOPARD

THE KEEPING ROOM

ANNA MYERS

ETHAN

BETWEEN

US

WALKER AND COMPANY

NEW YORK

First published in the United States of America in 1998 by
Walker Publishing Company, Inc.

Published simultaneously in Canada by Thomas Allen &
Son Canada, Limited, Markham, Ontario

Library of Congress Cataloging-in-Publication Data
Myers, Anna.
Ethan between us/Anna Myers.
p.   cm.
Summary: In an Oklahoma oil drilling camp in 1960,
fifteen-year-old Clare finds her relationship with her
best friend threatened by her new romance with Ethan,
a boy carrying a dark secret.
ISBN 0-8027-8670-7 (hardcover)
[1. Friendship—Fiction.   2. Mentally
ill—Fiction.   3. Oklahoma—Fiction.]   I. Title.
PZ7.M9814Et   1998
[Fic]—dc21   98-10697
CIP
AC

BOOK DESIGN BY JENNIFER ANN DADDIO

Printed in the United States of America

2   4   6   8   10   9   7   5   3   1

With love for Vanda Lee Hoover,
who is my brother,
and for Dr. Charles Biggers,
who is my brother in the law
and in the heart.

ONE

This is what I remember about Ethan. Sunflowers. There were sunflowers all over the cow pastures that surround the oil wells. And the smell of oil. Just about anyplace in Collins Creek, Oklahoma, a person's nose got filled up with that smell. The company poured oil on the red roads to calm the dust, or in case of rain, to fight the terrible crimson mud that could stop a gauger's pickup when he came to measure what the well produced.

We waited for rain that summer, but it didn't come. The sun turned into a giant oven and baked those lease roads that crisscrossed our community. The smell of hot black oil filled the air.

Now it is only May. Summer has not yet come to Oklahoma. Today I graduate from high school. Probably

I should be going over the speech I will make as the class valedictorian, but instead my thoughts are filled with Ethan.

I can close my eyes now and go back to that day in July, almost three years ago. There are sunflowers and the smell of oil. And there is Ethan. His family moved into one of the houses in our camp. Don't go thinking that we live in tents or something, but everyone calls this place the camp. We do have houses, twelve white ones that are just alike, arranged in a semicircle. In the middle, sort of common ground, there is a playground with a boss's office and sheds for equipment and the pipe yard down toward the gate.

There are three camps in Collins Creek. Some of the company workers have houses that sit off by them-selves on land leased from farmers. I am glad I don't live in one of the other camps or on a lease. If I did, Ethan would be just a boy that came to my school for a while.

Until Ethan it was just Liz and me against the world. I can't even remember a time before I knew Liz. We started school together, holding hands, at the redbrick building one mile down from our camp.

It wasn't like other people were unfriendly, but way back there we learned that the girls we knew were divided into two groups. There was us in one group, and the rest of them in the other.

The easiest way to explain this is to tell about the slumber party Jeannie Marie Tipton had in seventh grade. "Let's get in a circle and take turns telling about how we want our futures," somebody said, and Jeannie Marie went first because it was her party.

"After high school I'll probably work in Edmond and save money for my wedding. Of course, I'll have to buy a car, maybe a Chevy convertible. In about a year I'll get married." She paused to blow a big bubble, sucked back in the gum, and went on. "I might marry Gary Don Stoner or maybe my boss if he is cute. Then in two years I'll have twins, a boy named Mitch and a girl named Millie. We'll live in a brick house and go to Carlsbad Caverns on a vacation."

Liz was next. Of course, I knew what she would say, but I listened real close anyway because I liked hearing it. "I'll go to college somewhere with a really good dance program. I may not stay four years, not if I can get into a top-notch ballet company. And eventually I'll dance in cities everywhere, maybe even in Europe."

"Aren't you going to get married?" Jeannie Marie wanted to know.

Liz shrugged. "Maybe someday, but not at first."

"You'll be too old to have kids," Jeannie Marie warned.

"I'll dance," Liz said, and someone giggled.

It was my turn. For a minute I considered just passing, saying I didn't know what I wanted, which was partly true, but they had laughed at Liz. A scene from the story about the Alamo came to my mind. The line was drawn right there in Jeannie Marie's bedroom, just like it was drawn at the Alamo. I had to cross the line and stand with Liz.

"It's college for me too," I said. "I'm not sure what I'll do after college, but it will be something special. I can feel it sometimes like it is out there just waiting for me." I decided to block any questions. "I won't get married until I'm at least thirty, maybe later."

"You two have some really weird ideas," Julie Horton said while she put red polish on her big toenail. "I mean, I used to say I would be a movie star, but that was kid stuff. I mean, I'm thirteen, and my mother was married at sixteen."

The line separating us from the other girls got noticed by the boys too. Most of them still smiled at us in the halls. Hadn't we played ball with them in elementary school? But they didn't whistle at us, and when we walked down the school halls, we didn't change the way we moved even if they were standing there watching.

We didn't care. We had each other. And so we could laugh, and we did at almost anything. That summer afternoon of Ethan's coming the joke was mostly about the song title, "Only the Lonely." We had just discovered that I had misunderstood the words, and now we giggled about it.

"One, two, three," I said beginning to hum. "Phony Baloney," we sang. "Phony Baloney."

Then Liz put on her recital music, and she started to practice. Stretched on her bed, I watched her gliding around the room on her toes. One charm-braceleted arm caught and held my attention as it moved perfectly to the music.

The feeling I'd had off and on all summer started creeping back into me, all restless and wishing that I had a special dream like Liz did.

She whirled around me, her golden hair piled on top of her head, and I could see her dancing off to a dazzling future. My dreams didn't have any steps laid out for me to follow. She was all grace, and I was all misfit.

My dark hair was too curly, and compared to Liz I

moved like a boy. Sometimes I thought life would be easier if I were a boy, able really to belong to the world of leases and derricks. A girl in Collins Creek contributed only by washing her father's greasy coveralls. A boy my age would soon be able to work as a swabber, cleaning the rigs during the summer, and would have a place after graduation as a roustabout. I envied those laughing, bare-chested young men who passed by, casually perched on the back of the company trucks. I envied their camaraderie, their easy place in the world.

That was the thing. Until Ethan came, I didn't really have a place in the world. My feet were tough enough to walk barefoot on the hot creosote lease roads, but I felt only a little superior to the cows. I could cross the pipes of a cattle guard on foot, but I could never cross them on the back of a Sohio Company truck. I would never wear steel-toed shoes or a steel hat as protection from falling objects or thoughts from the outside world.

Now let me tell about how it was when I first saw Ethan. I should say when *we* saw Ethan, because Liz was with me, but the truth is, I have to think hard to remember that she was there.

The new people moved in next door to Liz while she had her dance lesson in Edmond. Her mother drove her, and I went along to go to the library. We didn't expect them to come that day. Liz, of course, would have gone to her lesson anyway, but I might have stayed home. We didn't get new people very often. See, that's how it was, Liz with a purpose and me with nothing important to do.

I went on home to eat as soon as we got back from Edmond, but I said I'd come back to Liz's as soon as supper was over, and I did. The evening meal was mostly finished for everyone by then, and the kids were already back outside. The little ones at the playground abandoned a game of Red Rover and started to toss balls over rooftops and call, "Ante over." Liz's dad had just finished turning a freezer of peach ice cream. We both got a bowl and went out to sit on her front porch. There were no curtains on the neighbor's living room window, and we could see right into it.

A boy came in and took a box off a piano. "Gosh, he's good-looking," said Liz.

He sat down on the bench. "Is he going to play?" I asked. We didn't know a single boy in Collins Creek who played the piano.

I guess I knew right at that first minute that we had never known anyone like Ethan Bennington. The music moved up through his hands and out into the summer twilight. It reached way down inside of me.

When Liz poked me in the side, I jumped, because I had sort of forgotten about her. "Do you think he knows we're out here? Maybe he's playing for us."

I shook my head. "I don't think he even knows the world's out here. Not when he plays like that."

TWO

That first night I put my pillow right on the sill of the window beside my bed and listened hard. Maybe the new boy had started to play again. I heard a dog bark down by the highway, and I could hear Jack Paar's voice from the neighbor's television. Mostly I heard the beat of the pump on a nearby oil well. The new boy's house was too far away. Liz would be able to open her window and listen. I felt sort of jealous for a minute, but it did not linger. No, I would not want him next door to me. The music of the oil well was more familiar, and I fell asleep to its rhythm.

"Clare." Mom woke me the next morning. She pushed open my door. "I need laundry soap," she said. "Would you mind?"

A quick bicycle trip to Griffith's store a mile down the road was a common chore for us older camp kids because most families only had one car. My dad's position meant he had a company pickup to drive to work, but our Chevy sat undisturbed in the driveway. My mom had never learned to drive because machines scared her.

Usually Liz and I made trips to the store together, and I got off my bike to knock on her door, but I didn't. From inside came the sound of Liz's recital music. She was practicing her ballet already.

I turned away from the door and went back to my bike. Actually, I did not mind being alone. Liz would have wanted to talk about the new boy, and I did not feel up to the discussion. I pumped hard on my bicycle's wheels.

It would be strange having a boy our age in the camp, a very good-looking boy. Lately boys made me feel sort of uneasy, especially good-looking ones. My last real boyfriend was back in third grade. Phil Watson was his name. We were so close we even pulled each other's loose teeth at recess. The affair began to slip downhill, though, when I tried to pull one of his teeth that wasn't even loose. Anyway, the next year his father got transferred to a different oil field.

I wouldn't think about boys anymore. Basketball was safe. I would think about basketball. I was glad Mom had woken me early. The sun had not yet begun its endless summer attempt at melting the asphalt highway. I could ride fast without danger of a heatstroke. I would go at it as hard as possible and mark in my mind the spot where I had to slow my pace. Tomorrow I would make it farther, and the next day even farther, eventually reaching the store without slacking. That way I would be prepared for the laps around the gym, conditioning for basketball season.

Liz and I both had hopes for being a main stringer in the fall because Shirley Leonard had graduated in the spring. We had decided to try hard to beat each other, being happy to let the coach decide.

After I eased up on the pedals, I began to notice things. Among the sheep in McGuire's pasture was a cute new black lamb, and I spotted two terrapins on the road. For a minute I felt the old urge to capture them. During earlier summers Liz and I had organized terrapin races in the camp. Collecting the terrapins, we would sell them to the smaller kids for ten cents each. A fifteen-cent fee allowed entry in our derby; leaving a profit even after we gave a fifty-cent prize. Once we had visions of really big money and started accepting bets on the winner. The future looked bright until my mother got wind of it all. "Baptists," she had said, staring pointedly at Liz, who is a Catholic, "don't even gamble on horses. No child of mine is about to start with turtles."

Remembering produced a great longing inside me, and I got off my bike and moved one of the terrapins because it was in the middle of the road. If only I could gather up the terrapins and somehow ride backward on my bike to the days of yesteryear, as they say on *The Lone Ranger*. Only I didn't want to go quite that far. Three or four years would do it. Then I could live the good life again, simple and unperplexed.

Except for the church, Collins Creek's one claim to fame, a traveler might not notice our little settlement at all. The pipes that made the frame for the giant tepee came from the oil field. The farmers seem to think of the school as theirs and dominate the school board, but the church definitely says, "Oil." It was built by the men on Saturdays and evenings after full days of work. With the women serving supper and the little kids playing hide-and-seek or blindman's bluff, the church raising seemed like a great, long party.

At Griffith's store across the street from the church

there was only a Coca-Cola sign. Collins Creek, made up of the one small grocery, a school, and the Baptist church, doesn't need signs of identification. We don't even have a post office. Our address is Route 2, Edmond, and it is to that town twelve miles away that the people of Collins Creek drive for serious grocery shopping and stuff.

Caps from pop bottles covered Griffith's driveway to keep cars from sinking into ruts during spring or fall rains. Just to occupy my mind, I looked down for Royal Crown caps as I walked to the door. All those caps. How many were from my years of drinking pop at Collins Creek's combination gas station, grocery store, hamburger stand, and social center? How many more bottles would I drink before I went away to some unknown future?

There was a distinctive, not unpleasant odor waiting just inside Griffith's. It came, probably, from the linoleum that covered the floor and counter and was mixed with the smell of onions, used on the hamburgers fixed at noontime.

On the first three stools sat men deep into an argument about whether Nixon or Kennedy would be elected in the fall. I collected the Tide detergent and settled myself at the far end of the counter. "Take out for a grape too," I said, and I handed a dollar bill to Mrs. Griffith, who, being uninterested in politics, hovered near me as I drank.

"New people get moved in up there, did they?" she inclined her head toward the camp.

"I guess so. Pretty much."

"Got a boy, don't they?"

I nodded.

"How come Liz isn't with you this morning?"

"Practicing," I said, and it was Mrs. Griffith's turn to nod. Liz's great enthusiasm for ballet was well known. In Collins Creek such passion marked her as odd. I was probably considered odd too, but the reason was not as clear.

When Jess Russell came in, I paid the three-cent deposit allowing me to take the bottle of grape pop. I had to get out of there before he came to sit beside me and lean his leg against mine like it was an accident. He was older than my father and the leader of my Sunday night Training Union class, where the week before he had put his hand caressingly on my shoulder during a Bible sword drill. Not only had I been unable to find Psalms 120:4, I had very nearly thrown up on God's Holy Word.

"I sing because I'm happy" is a line from a song in our church hymnal, but when I sing, it is usually to drive out darkness. And so to rid my mind of Jess Russell, I belted out "I Am Resolved," all five verses, on the ride home.

Inside the camp gates, two trucks were parked near the tool dock. One was being loaded with equipment from the dock. Workers from the other were gathered around the icehouse, filling water cans with hunks of ice. I felt sort of shy riding by the men and kept my eyes down. When I lifted them, it was to see Liz's house.

The sight made me put on the brakes quickly. Sitting there on the front porch talking, looking into each other's faces, were Liz and Ethan Bennington.

Go on over to them, some reasonable part of my mind said. "Not on your life," I answered aloud. Turning back, I took the long way around to my house, riding on the other side of the tool house and avoiding Liz's house completely.

What's wrong with you? The reasonable voice tried again. Why are you acting so sappy? This time I made no reply. Inside the house, I handed my mother the detergent and, without waiting to be asked, picked up a basket of wet wash and went out to hang it up.

The sun was warm on my back as I bent to take laundry from the basket. In the backyard cottonwood a bird warbled. I opened my mouth to sing, but I couldn't find any words.

One line was full when I saw Liz running toward me through the neighbor's backyard, all graceful and fair just like the gazelles I had seen on the educational channel the other day. I could imagine music playing, Ethan's music.

When Liz slowed to a walk, I went on with the clothes, acting as if I hadn't been watching her at all.

"Clare," she called, and I felt ashamed of the urge to wrap my little brother's jeans around her neck instead of pinning them to the line.

"What's new?" I stopped work and looked at her.

"Well," Liz said, and she reached for a towel and started hanging it up, "I met Ethan Bennington."

"Really?" This is crazy, I told myself. Why am I acting this way? I picked up Mom's apron.

"Yeah," Liz said from around the clothespin she was holding in her mouth. "He's nice."

The laundry was finished. There was nothing to do but ask her inside. Get hold of yourself, the reasonable voice said.

Inside, I fixed glasses of iced tea and took Liz into

my room. "Tell me about him." I thought my tone sounded pretty normal.

"Well," Liz paused and wrinkled her nose like she does when she is thinking. "It's funny. He's different. Real easy to talk to."

"What did you talk about?"

"He ran his finger up my nose."

I stared at her. His finger up her nose! Had Liz lost her mind? How could someone who played the piano like he did be weird enough to want his finger in someone's nose? It made me sick, and Liz could see I didn't understand.

"Like this," she said, putting her finger on the end of her nose and tracing it to her forehead.

"Oh," was all I said.

"That's funny. You thought he put his finger in my nose." Liz was ready to laugh, and she looked at me, waiting for me to laugh too. "I haven't heard anything so funny since 'Phony Baloney.'"

I wanted to giggle with Liz. I really did, but I just couldn't. I even thought of bringing up Phil Watkins. Maybe I would remind Liz of my reputation with men and ask if Ethan had any loose teeth. I didn't though. I just asked, "What did he say?" Like I cared.

"He said I have a cute nose. He just said 'Hi.' Then he touched my nose like that and said it was cute."

"Weren't you embarrassed?" I let my voice show that she certainly should have been.

"No," Liz began to do ballet movements around my room, so I stretched across the bed. "That's what I mean. He's different. I can't explain it, but I just felt real comfortable."

What bothered me was why I felt so uncomfortable, but I made myself ask the expected question. "What else happened?"

"Not much, really. I asked him if he wanted to play Monopoly with you and me this afternoon. I'm really anxious for you to meet him."

I wasn't anxious, not at all. "I've got to do laundry most of the day," I blurted out.

Liz shrugged. "It doesn't matter. Ethan has to help his mother put stuff away and all anyway. Oh, yeah, he told me that he's seventeen, just had his birthday, but he'll only be a junior."

"Guess he flunked a year." Suddenly I felt like making the bed. Jumping up, I pulled at the chenille bedspread until Liz took the other end and helped me smooth it across the bed.

When we were finished, Liz reached out to touch my arm. "What's wrong? You seem sort of down."

I turned away to look out the window. "Oh, nothing, really. Guess just the summer-bored blues. And I kind of wish sometimes that I had something to care about the way you do dancing."

Liz put her arm around my shoulder. "You're the smartest kid in our class. You'll do great things and be adored." I shrugged, and Liz went on. "And phony baloney, you'll never be lonely. Remember our rock?"

Just two summers earlier we had written our names and "friends forever" on a big sandstone and thrown it into Johnson's pond.

"I know I've got the best friend in the world." I gave her a real smile. "Tell you what, why don't we make a picnic lunch tomorrow and go out to our old hideout in the woods?"

"Yeah." Liz began to pirouette around the room. "Maybe we should invite Ethan, what do you think?"

I pushed down a sigh. "Sure, why not." I had to face the fact that Ethan Bennington would be part of our summer.

THREE

The thing with Liz's aunt happened next. Looking back, I wonder about how different that summer might have been if it hadn't been for Liz's aunt.

I really did spend most of that day on the laundry, using the stick to push Dad's greasy work clothes into the hot churning suds, hanging up everything, taking it all down, sprinkling for ironing, folding, and putting away.

All that work made me tired and made Mom grateful. She kept telling me I could quit and go over to Liz's or something, but I didn't. So when I said I was too tired for Wednesday night prayer meeting, Mom said I could stay home.

I had just reached for the peanut butter to make

myself a sandwich when the knock came, and then before I could get to the door I heard Liz's voice. "Clare, let me in. I've only got just a minute."

As soon as I opened the door, I saw the tears on Liz's cheeks. "Mom wants me right back home to help get our clothes ready and some extra stuff done around the house. We're leaving in the morning first thing. Mom, me, and Linda are going to Arkansas. Aunt Virginia has got to stay in bed, or else her baby will come too early."

"Don't cry." I put my hand on Liz's shoulder. Her aunt Virginia, her mom's younger sister, was real special to Liz. Virginia had a little girl that Liz loved a lot too. "Your aunt will be okay and the baby too, I bet."

"Oh, I know it." She wiped at her eyes. "But the phone call scared us, and Aunt Virginia was crying. Besides, I don't know. I just hate to be gone all summer."

I knew what she meant, but I didn't say so. "Really? I'd love to go somewhere."

Liz wiped at her tears. "Well, there's my recital practices, of course. But then I pretty much know the routine, and I can practice every day. Maybe I won't get too far behind." She smiled a little. "Come on, walk home with me."

At first I had to almost trot to stay up with Liz, but

I noticed a big change in pace as we got near her house. She stopped just before we reached it, and we stood on the gravel road. "Gosh." Liz looked past her home toward the one at the end. "I was thinking we might really have some fun with Ethan. Of course, you can still get to know him. I'm sure you'll like him."

I turned away from the house out toward Johnson's pasture. Just then Mrs. Teal came to the door. "Liz, honey," she called, "you've got to come on in and help."

I reached out to give Liz a quick hug. "Don't worry," I said, but suddenly the music started. There were shades on the window, but we knew Ethan was playing the piano. It was the same melody as the night before, haunting and beautiful.

"Oh!" Liz wailed into her handkerchief. Then she flung herself toward the house.

"It'll be all right," I said, but I didn't say it loud enough to be heard over the music that surrounded me. Without intending to, I took a few steps toward the Bennington house. Go home, I thought, but I didn't move. If Liz looked out the window, she would see me standing in the twilight, unable to move because Ethan Bennington played the piano.

I have to think carefully to know that the time of

listening in the shadows was not long. Ethan's playing stopped soon, but in my mind it seems much longer, one of those forever moments frozen in my memory like a sweet smile caught in an old snapshot. It has come back to me often, especially on summer evenings.

When the music ended, I made my way home slowly, looking at each house like unfamiliar territory. I didn't go inside, just sat on the porch steps and waited for my family. A heavy loneliness filled me. "It's because Liz is going away," I said to the night, but I knew that was a lie. It was the music.

FOUR

This is the part that gets hard to tell because it is the part where Ethan stops being just the new boy who plays beautiful music and becomes—? See, that's the hard part to put into words. How can I explain what Ethan came to mean to me? I sure don't want anyone thinking this is one of those drippy love stories. There is a lot more to it than that.

It starts with Ethan and me at the playground. I didn't know he was there. I woke up before six o'clock, which is awful early for me. Right off I wondered if Liz had left yet for Arkansas, so I got up and sat by my east window, because from there I could see the spot where the Teal's car would leave their driveway and be visible on the main camp drive. Sure enough, the familiar blue Ford came into view in just a minutes.

Dad wasn't even up and shaving yet, and Mom wasn't in the kitchen making his daily pancakes. I didn't feel sleepy anymore, so I took a book of poetry out to the playground. The grass was still wet from the dew, and the air had a cool, fresh feel to it. In the mulberry tree a group of black birds seemed to be holding a convention. My English teacher, Franklin T. Elliot, believes poetry ought to be read aloud, and I pretty much agree. I stretched out on a damp bench and got really into "If." I was on my favorite part about the game of pitch and toss when the dog licked me in the face.

"No, King," said his master. "My name's Ethan," he said. "I bet you're Clare. Liz told me you like to read, and you sound good doing it."

I sat up. He likes the way I read. Next he'll like my nose too. Maybe I should tell him to keep his finger out of it, but I didn't. "It's poetry," I said and then felt stupid, pointing out the obvious. I started petting the dog.

"Do you like dogs?" He sat down on the bench beside me.

I nodded. "We used to have a collie sort of like this one, but he got run over."

"You never got another one?"

"My little brother wants to, but I don't." I glanced up at him, and there was something about the way he looked at me. I heard myself telling all about Old Sunny. How his body was on the edge of the highway, and someone on the bus yelled out that everyone should look at the dead dog. Liz told whoever it was to shut his stupid mouth. When we got off, I ran to my dog, hoping he wasn't dead, but he was. Liz pulled me up away from him and carried my books home. I was glad Teddy had the chicken pox and wasn't on the bus.

When I finished the story, I started to be embarrassed again for blurting it all out, but another look at Ethan made me stop. I wish I could explain his expression, like he understood everything I said. No, it was more than understood. It was like he felt everything I said.

I jumped up. "Mom will panic if she finds my bed empty at this hour and thinks I've been stolen away in the night or something."

"You don't usually get up early, huh?" He stood too, and I knew he planned to walk home with me.

"Not in summer. Do you?"

"Oh." He paused to pull a little blue berry from a

cedar tree. "Lots of times I can't sleep." He shrugged. "I don't really mind. There's so much to do."

"Are you kidding?" I asked, but I could tell he wasn't. Didn't he know about the hot and forever summer days in Oklahoma oil fields? After all, we weren't exactly in New York City. Besides it didn't seem right to say you weren't bored. It was like admitting a fondness for food in the school cafeteria. No kid would do that even if the food happened to be good.

"Time always seems short to me," he said with another shrug, and he turned around to walk backward for a few steps, facing me.

"I heard you play the piano last night and the night before. It was beautiful."

"Do you like music?" There was an eagerness in his voice, and he stopped walking again, waiting for my answer.

I wanted to say I loved it, had always loved it. I made my voice show my apology. "I don't know anything about the kind of music you play. I don't even listen to the radio close like Liz does. Would you believe I actually thought the song "Only the Lonely" was "Phony Baloney"?

We both laughed then, and I liked it, which was

strange because I had never enjoyed a joke on myself with anyone except Liz.

In front of my house, I bent down to pet King again because I didn't want to go in.

"Liz said something about the three of us playing Monopoly," he said.

I didn't look up from the dog. "We can't, though. Liz had to go to Arkansas with her mother and little sister. She's going to be gone for a while."

"Well, then, we'll have to find something just the two of us can do," he said. "Tell you what. I don't know much about poetry. You teach me about poetry this summer, and I'll teach you about serious music."

It was like I was almost afraid to turn my face up to see him, not just because he was handsome with his square shoulders, dark hair, and all. It was the tenderness in his eyes, like he loved me because I was part of a beautiful world and like maybe he could make me see all that beauty.

"It's a deal," I said.

"How about we start this afternoon? After lunch I'll come back over, okay?"

"Sounds good," I straightened up, took a last pat at King's head, turned, and ran inside. I did not look over my shoulder at him; instead I kept my eyes on the green wooden steps and then on the front porch. Just before I opened the door, I let myself glance back. He walked quickly, and the blue of his shirt matched the sky.

Mom heard the door open and stepped into the living room. "My goodness, have you been out already, dear?"

"Sure," I said. "I don't want to just sleep my summer away." Then I surprised her even more by fixing myself, who never liked breakfast, a big plate of bacon and eggs.

All morning I went from one activity to another. In my room I picked up a book I had been excited about bringing home from the library, but on page two I put it down. I started to clean, but after I made the bed and dusted the dresser, it looked good enough.

My soap opera didn't hold my attention, even though the heroine was about to have her wedding interrupted by a husband who was supposed to have died in a plane crash. I sat on the couch and stared at the screen, but I didn't notice whether the wedding came off or not. My thoughts were full of Ethan.

Don't get all excited about this boy, I warned myself. Sure he's friendly now, but he's seventeen. Things will change later when he meets the older kids. Give him a few days, and he'll be driving all around Collins Creek, probably with a car full of girls. Dad wouldn't let me go anywhere with him even if he asked. Maybe it would be better to just give him the brush-off if he really comes over here later.

At lunch Mom told me and Teddy that the garden needed weeding. "You can wait till after supper, though, when it's cooler."

When the dishes were cleared away, I went out back. "You can do your part later," I told Teddy. I didn't tell him that chopping weeds would keep me from hanging around the window watching for Ethan.

When I looked up from the tomatoes to see Ethan coming around the corner of my house, I swiped at the sweat on my face with my hand and glanced down at the pair of old cut-off jeans. Maybe I should have dressed better. No, if he's going to be around regularly, he might as well see the real me.

"Want some help?" he asked.

"No, Mom thinks it's too hot to work out here long." I went to the outside hydrant, turned on the water, and washed my hands. I hoped he would mention the music lesson, and he did.

"Let's head for my house, then. Music time." He turned the water off for me.

On the way we talked about school, and what his classes would be. There's not a bunch of course offerings at Collins Creek. I figured Ethan would be unhappy about that, coming from Dallas, but he didn't seem to mind.

At his house Mrs. Bennington stood in the doorway, and I had the feeling she might have been watching for us. Like Ethan, she was tall and dark. She gave me a big smile, but her eyes didn't seem to know about the smile. She looked sort of worried, and I figured the move must have got her down.

"Oh, I'm so glad Ethan will have friends here in the camp." She turned to her son. "That's what you need, young people to talk to. I'll fix lemonade after a bit," she promised, and then she left us alone in the living room.

"Sit with me on the bench." Ethan took a stack of music from the piano.

"I know what I want to hear first," I told him. "That one you played your first night here. Liz and I listened from the front porch, and I heard it again last night."

He stopped looking through the music. "Oh, I don't

play that piece very often." A small frown formed on his lips. "Maybe I'll do it for you another time." He chose a sheet of music and put the stack back on the piano. "How about the *Warsaw Concerto*?"

I felt a little disappointed, but when he began to play, I wondered how I could have hoped for another piece. On his finger was a ring with a red stone. It was his birthstone, he told me later, given to him by his grandmother last year for his sixteenth birthday.

The light was caught by that red stone, and so was the moment. The ring is mine now. Whenever I hold it in my hand, I am back beside Ethan on that piano bench, and the *Warsaw Concerto* fills the room.

Mrs. Bennington came in just as the music stopped. She carried a tray with glasses of lemonade. "Maybe you two would like to watch some television," she said. Ethan shook his head. I thought his mother was going to say something else, but instead she just sort of bit at her lip and went back out of the room.

I took my lemonade right away, but Ethan ignored his and went on playing. I thought some of the notes sounded like the piece I had heard before. Maybe he would play it for me after all.

But Mrs. Bennington marched back into the room. "Well," she said as she came in. "Why don't you children play a nice game of Clue." Her words sounded more like an order than a suggestion. I noticed her hand shook when she held out the box to her son. "I'm sure Clare is tired of the piano, and besides, I need a nap. You've practiced enough today anyway, Ethan. You need to relax."

A look passed between Ethan and his mother, and I felt sort of uneasy. I stood up. "I'd better go," I said.

"Wait." Ethan took the game from his mother. "We'll go out on the porch."

I wondered what had changed Mrs. Bennington from the friendly woman who had held the door for me.

"Mom thinks I practice too much," Ethan said when we were on the porch. I sat right down on the steps, but Ethan just stood there, kind of going up and down on the balls of his feet. "Dad too. Sometimes I have this wild fear that I'll come home from school or something and the piano will be gone."

"They wouldn't do a thing like that! Surely not! Aren't they proud? Don't they know you're something special?"

He gave me a sort of weak little grin. "My folks never planned to have a son who'd get all wrapped up in music."

"Why? They had to get you the lessons. Right?"

He grinned again. "My grandma had an old piano. I started playing on it, way before I went to school. Grandma gave me the piano, paid for my lessons. My folks were never really into it much, especially my dad. Mom didn't mind that much until—" He paused. "Oh, I am sure you're not interested in all of this."

"I am." I wanted to put my arm around him. "That's not an old piano in there."

"Grandma again. She bought it for me."

"Do you take lessons?"

He shook his head. "Dad said no more." He shrugged, "He says there's no one to teach me. I'm pretty sure we could find someone." He rubbed the back of his neck. "I won't quit playing. I won't."

I studied my hands, trying to think of something to make him feel better. "I can't understand. What's wrong with your dad?"

"Oh, he's not so bad really. He's good to me in other ways. There are things—" Again he paused. Then his face brightened, like he had thought of a way to explain. "He's not so much different from other guys around here, I guess. Take your dad. Would he want your little brother to be so deep into piano playing?"

I traced the lines of the boards in the porch. "I don't know," I said. "Maybe he wouldn't." Just then I turned and caught a glimpse of Mrs. Bennington looking out the window, and I remembered my mother's warning about how Teddy and I shouldn't wear out our welcomes at other people's houses. I didn't want to go, but I forced myself to say that I had to.

"I'm afraid our lessons didn't get off to a very good start. I won't dump my problems on you next time." He smiled and started down the steps with me. "We'll do poetry tomorrow, right?" He seemed relaxed again, and it was clear he intended to walk me home.

Out on the road, I picked up a piece of gravel and made a good throw over to the center strip near the tool shed. "Bet you can't beat that," I challenged.

He wound up like a pitcher, but his rock fell far short. "I thought you girls let guys win at things like that," he teased.

"No, sir." I threw another rock. "Not Liz or me. We are what my grandmother calls 'emancipated women.'"

"You'll miss Liz this summer, I guess."

Suddenly I did, and I felt bad that I hadn't thought about her once all day. "I'd better go in," I told Ethan.

"See you tomorrow," he said, and his smile made me forget the guilt over Liz.

Mom was in the living room. "Getting to know the new boy?" she asked when I came through the door.

"Yeah." I went into the kitchen for a glass of ice water, and my mother followed, ready for more information. I chose my words carefully. "I think we're going to be good friends." Only fear of protesting too much kept me from adding, "Just good friends." I had suddenly realized that my dad, who always said no dating until I was sixteen, might not even let me hang around the camp with Ethan.

Mom didn't seem to mind, just smiled. "That's nice, honey. I must go over and take them some cookies or something soon."

That night after supper I went to my room to write to Liz. I wanted to tell her all about being with Ethan Bennington at his house, about his parents not wanting him to play the piano, and about the strange feeling that was growing inside me about this new boy. I sat for a long time with my pen in hand and my writing pad on my desk. Maybe it wouldn't be right to tell Liz about Ethan's problems with his parents. But hadn't we always told each other everything? How could I be more loyal to this boy I hardly knew than to Liz? Finally, I gave up and went in to take a shower. I'd write to Liz tomorrow.

FIVE

On the second day of knowing Ethan Bennington, I was already different. I woke up early again, but this time I didn't even try to go back to sleep. I remembered what he said about having so much to do, and I felt that way too.

Maybe Ethan waited outside for me right now. I slipped out the front door. From the playground in the middle of the camp I could see the Bennington house. Settling myself on top of the picnic table, I watched Mr. Bennington leave for work. He wasn't as dark as Ethan and his mother, and not as good-looking. He got into a gray Nash Rambler and drove away. A newer blue Ford still sat in the driveway.

Two cars were unusual. At seventeen, Ethan was bound to have a driver's license. He'd be doing errands for his mother. Surely I would be allowed to ride with him down to Griffith's. Smiling, I let myself imagine how it would be, me in the seat beside Ethan, the windows open, blowing our hair, and the radio playing. "Stop it," I said aloud. "Dad would never let you spend the summer driving around with a boy."

There was dust on the tabletop. "Clare," I wrote. Then I looked around to make sure I was alone and added "Ethan" beside it.

For another thirty minutes I stayed at the playground. For a while I swung and tried to sing "Only the Lonely," but I could not remember many of the words. Then I wandered over to the fence and spent some time touching and smelling the climbing roses. Finally I figured I'd better go in or Mom might come out looking for me. I took a leaf from the mulberry tree and used it to erase the names I had written on the table.

The morning dragged just like it had the day before. I tried hard not to think about Ethan coming over. I even asked Teddy to play a game of checkers with me at the kitchen table. He won without me giving him any advantages. "You're not so sharp today," he said. "Got your mind on that Ethan guy, I bet." I made a face at him and didn't offer to help put the game away.

Finally I let myself go to my room to read poetry and mark pages I wanted to share with Ethan. By noon I was nervous. Maybe I had dreamed up the specialness of the day before. Maybe Ethan wouldn't come at all or would come only later when he couldn't find anything better to do.

When Teddy announced he was hungry, I heard him. "I'll fix lunch," I called from my room, glad for some reason to move about.

My mother was in the kitchen, stirring up a cake for supper. "You seem nervous, Clare," she commented when I dropped the mustard jar for the second time. "Is something on your mind?"

"No," I shook my head, but I did not look at Mom when I put the onion, unused, back in the vegetable bin. I love onions on my sandwiches, but a poetry teacher shouldn't have onion breath.

When lunch was over and the dishes washed and put away, I could stand it no longer. "Think I'll ride down to the store for exercise," I told my mother. "I've got to get in shape for basketball. Need anything?"

"No." Mom settled on the couch for a rest. "I'd rather you put off your exercise until after the sun goes down or until tomorrow morning early. They're talking about heatstrokes on the news."

"I'll just ride around the camp once, then," I said and hurried out the door before my mother could object. Outside I took my bike and rode slowly toward Ethan's house. The gravel crunched under the tires and seemed loud in the quiet afternoon. I hoped Ethan would come out, but what would I say if he did?

Even before I reached Liz's house, I heard the piano. Music filled the road around his house. The notes bounced into the sun, not the *Warsaw Concerto* or the special piece I had first heard him play, but wonderful lively music.

I put on my brakes and dropped my feet onto the road, where I stood holding on to the handlebars until a car came up behind me and honked its horn. Mr. Hill, who lives next door to me, sat behind the wheel. What was he doing home on a Friday afternoon, driving around disturbing people with all that honking? But I had to admit he had the right of way. I pushed my bike to the side of the road.

Maybe I would just put down the bike and go sit on

the Bennington's porch. But how would I feel if someone came out? Then an idea came to me. Liz's house was right next door, and with her father at work, no one was home. I could sit there and listen to Ethan play.

The porch swing was perfect, shady and out of sight. I stretched out only a few feet from the open window of the Bennington home. The hedge hid me from view, and I could lie there, eyes closed, and drift with the music.

He played and played, pausing only briefly between the end of one piece and the beginning of the next.

I relaxed completely, floating with the music, but the playing stopped suddenly and a voice came instead. "It's only been a little over thirty minutes. We agreed on an hour." Ethan's tone sounded agitated.

His mother's voice answered. Straining to hear, I put a foot to the porch to stop the swing's creaking movement, but I still couldn't make out Mrs. Bennington's words.

Ethan spoke again, this time with an easier tone. "I know, Mama. I know you worry, but I wish you wouldn't. It wasn't the piano playing that made me sick. Remember, even Dr. Smithers told you that. I'm fine, Mama. The bad times are over."

Eavesdropping. That's what I was doing. What if Ethan saw me? Lying perfectly still on the swing, I hardly breathed. Ethan did not go back to the music. Was he sitting on the piano bench? What if he came outside?

Finally, after it had been quiet for a while, I eased up and peeked over the edge of the hedge. No one stirred at the Benningtons'. I made a dash for my bike.

At home I went into the bathroom, glad to be alone. Washing my face, I stared into the mirror and went back over every word I had heard. What did Ethan mean about being sick? Fear started to get its cold fingers on me. I shook my head. "You've only known him two days," I whispered to my reflection. "You can't care about him all that much." I gazed closely at the girl in the mirror and knew she was a liar.

When he came to my door about thirty minutes later, his smile did not seem to belong to a boy who had been very ill. "I'm ready, teacher," he said.

I was ready too, and we went to the backyard with poetry books and a blanket to spread under the big cottonwood.

Ethan stretched on his back. I stacked the books between us and sat with my legs crisscrossed beneath me.

Nothing should look improper to my mother, who no doubt would look out at us from the kitchen window.

"I think we'll read 'Death of a Hired Man' first," I said. "It's by Robert Frost." I hadn't gotten very far when he sat up.

"You're hardly looking at the words." He reached for the book. "You've got this thing almost memorized."

I shrugged. "After I've read them over and over, I just sort of know them. Like you do music, I guess."

He shook his head. "Seems harder to me."

He took the book and let it fall open naturally. " 'Annabel Lee,' " he said. "Let's hear it."

I got about halfway through Poe's poem before he had to help me. "Do you ever write poetry?" he asked.

"Some." I watched the white fluff drift down from the cottonwood tree and tried to think of a way to change the subject.

"Will you let me see your poems?"

"Oh, I've never kept any. They're too dumb." I picked up a book, ready to read again.

"You need to have a journal, write your poems and your thoughts in it. I'll bet you'll be a writer someday."

Feeling a little embarrassed couldn't keep me from

smiling at him. Being a writer had crossed my mind before, but I had never talked about it, not even to Liz.

We went back to reading more poetry. Every little bit, I'd think about what I had overheard. I'd glance at Ethan and wonder what it all meant.

It seemed almost like he could read my mind, because I was thinking about his illness when he suddenly said, "I've been meaning to tell you why I'm seventeen and will just be a junior this year."

He sort of blurted it out, like he had to say it fast or not at all. For some reason I made a silly wisecrack. "Flunked last year and have to repeat, I bet."

When he nodded, I swallowed hard. "That's right," he said. "I missed most of the school year because I was real sick."

"Oh, gosh, I'm sorry." I thought he would go on to tell about his illness, and I wanted to hold my breath. What if he told me he had a terminal illness? I remembered how he had said something that first morning about time being short. "Sick enough to lose a whole year at school? Are you okay now? What was wrong?"

Ethan shook his head, and he didn't say anything for a second. Then he smiled. "Oh, it's not my favorite subject, but I'll tell you about it one of these days. Don't worry, though, I'm not going to be sick again."

I studied his face. He looked healthy, but there was something about the way he said the part about not being sick again, like I might say, "I can do ten laps around the gym," like his health might depend on his determination. I wanted more information, but I didn't push.

He started to get up, and I was afraid he would go home. "How about a glass of iced tea?" I asked. We went inside and ended up playing Monopoly with Teddy.

Ethan loved the game, and he got ahead pretty quickly. He laughed when he rolled the dice and landed on the best property. "Luck must be with me," he said stacking green houses on Boardwalk and Park Place. I sure hoped he was right.

SIX

Those summer days were perfect. My parents talked a lot about our need for rain, but the brown grass looked fine to me as long as I walked across it with Ethan. But I felt real bad about Liz, guilty I guess is the word, because deep down I hoped she stayed in Arkansas for a long time. Being with Ethan filled up my life. How could I make room for the person who was now, undeniably, my second-best friend?

When I finally got around to writing to Liz, I just said, "Ethan and I are really close. I just never would have believed a boy like him would move into our camp."

Liz's answer was quick. "There's lots you're not telling. Are you in love with Ethan Bennington?"

After that letter came, I thought about the question all afternoon. In the evening I went for a walk by myself through Johnson's pasture and back to the woods. I found the tree that Liz and I often climbed and shinnied up.

The pump of the nearby oil well was as familiar to me as the beating of my own heart. I pressed my hand against my chest to see if maybe my heart and the oil well had the same rhythm, and they really did seem to. I wondered about leaving this place, which would surely happen someday. If I went away to live in a different place, would my heart be able to beat on its own without the rhythm of that oil well?

And then I started thinking again about Liz's question. Leaning on one hip, I reached into the back pocket of my jeans for the letter. There it was: "Are you in love with Ethan Bennington?" For a long time I looked at the letters in Liz's neat blue words.

Liz and I had talked lots of times about love, mystical and far away, something that grabbed a girl up and made her feel like she floated with the clouds.

Sitting there in that tree, I had a vague idea that love might not be such a magic thing. It might happen a little at a time while a person just went on hoeing weeds and playing Monopoly. I smiled and drew in a deep breath. I would write to Liz that I didn't know for sure what being in love meant and was not about to claim to be in it.

One thing, though, I did know. Liz and I had often laughed at a necklace worn briefly during the last school year by a girl named Sheila Olsen, a silly girl a year ahead of us in school. It was heart-shaped and engraved with the word "Kenneth's." For a few weeks Sheila had faithfully worn the necklace, declaring to the world that she belonged to Kenneth.

We had snickered over the idea that one person could belong to another like an object. I did not for a minute believe Sheila understood the concept, but I could no longer laugh at the idea it represented. I would never engrave it on a necklace, but I knew for sure and certain that part of me belonged to Ethan Bennington. He might move to China next week. I might never see him again. I might grow up to marry a man I adore and with whom I might have a dozen children. Still, part of me would belong to Ethan Bennington, and part of him would be mine.

It wasn't something I could write to Liz. Instead, I decided, I would begin to keep a journal, like Ethan had suggested.

I climbed down from the tree and went home to write to Liz. "The Bennington kid came looking for you," my father told me when I walked through the living room. I could tell there was more, but I moved on toward my room. "Wait a minute," Dad said. "You do remember, don't you, that there won't be any dating until you're sixteen, and that's almost a year."

I nodded. "Maybe with luck, I'll convert to being a Catholic like Liz by then and decide to be a nun."

My father wasn't impressed with my humor. "Catholic or not, just don't you get in a car with that boy or any other and start off somewhere. Time enough for that later."

It was no problem. Ethan seemed neither to drive a car nor to talk of driving one. I admitted, only to myself, that it was a little strange. Other boys were either driving every chance they got or complaining because they got no chance.

"Do you ever drive your folk's car?" I asked one afternoon as we gave King a bath. In Oklahoma a collie with white on it requires frequent washing. Otherwise the white is permanently dyed red by the mud.

Ethan stopped rubbing and looked at me. "Why? Do you need to go somewhere?"

"No." I started to regret starting the conversation. "No. I was just wondering."

He scrubbed hard at the white hair under King's neck. "I haven't driven in a while because of the medicine I take. It's pretty strong."

"Oh," was all I said. Part of me wanted to jump into King's dirty bathwater and drown myself for bringing it up. Part of me wanted to have the courage to ask why, to find out all about the medicine and the illness he evidently was not completely recovered from.

Neither of us said anything for a while. I kept hoping Ethan would volunteer some information, but he didn't. Eventually he started telling me elephant jokes. Having heard Teddy tell them all to him the night before, I knew he was desperate to change the subject.

When the bath was finished, I wandered home. Ethan didn't try to talk me out of going.

It was just about to get dark that evening when I went out to sit on the porch. Fear lay heavy and unfamiliar inside me. My world, before Ethan, was dull but always safe. The illness that had kept him out of school for a year still had a hold on him. "There's such little time," I remembered again. Everything inside me turned to ice.

A house or two down, some kids were playing hide-

and-seek. I could hear them call, "Awllie awllie outs in free." A whippoorwill was mixing its cry with the beat of the oil pump. I could find no comfort in the familiar sounds or in the full, orange moon.

Somehow I knew Ethan would come, and he did, taking his place beside me on the step.

"What's new?" I asked.

He rubbed the back of his neck. "It isn't new, but I spent four months last winter in a mental hospital."

So that was it. Shock mixed with relief. He wasn't dying. People didn't die from being crazy. "Crazy," the word repeated in my mind. Staring at the moon, I said nothing.

"I'll bet you don't know many sure-enough nuts, do you?" he asked, trying to make a joke.

It was unavoidably my turn to speak. "No. You're the first."

He laughed, and I breathed deeply. Still, inside me the fear, now having a name, grew larger. Just then my mother came to the door to call me in. I stood before Ethan did and touched his shoulder for just a second. "See you tomorrow," was all I could say.

Inside I got ready for bed as quickly as I could and

said good night to the family. "I'm pretty tired," I told them. I wasn't really tired, but I needed to be alone.

They were watching *Have Gun, Will Travel* on television. Even with the door closed, I could hear the music.

"Crazy. Crazy. Crazy." I said to myself. The word did not fit Ethan, but it was, undeniably, the word for people who went to mental hospitals. After a while I stopped thinking of how strange it seemed to me and began dwelling on how it must have been for Ethan.

Crying until I really was very tired, I fell asleep while my folks were watching Wally Kannan, the weather man.

My mother woke me by touching my shoulder. It was almost light. "You were moaning, Clare. Are you okay?" She put her hand to my forehead to check for fever.

"Just a dream," I said, but I had no desire to go back to sleep. When the daylight finally came, I dressed and headed for the Benningtons', gathering tiny pebbles from the road to throw at Ethan's window. He pushed back the curtain right away and held up a finger to mean wait.

"Let's walk," he said. The morning seemed unusually beautiful, all golden and new. As we headed toward Johnson's pond, I wished we were only meandering, that no important discussion waited.

The pond could not have been described as a scenic spot. The water was Oklahoma-mud red. Cows, evidently indifferent to the color, had left hundreds of holes in the muddy edges where they had stood to drink.

"When we were younger," I told him, "Liz and I played here a lot and called this our Lake of Sparkling Water. We had real imaginations, huh?"

"You want to talk about when I was sick." He skipped a rock across the pond.

"Yes," I searched for words. "I mean, if it is okay."

"Sure," he said, but he turned away from the water, and we headed back toward our camp, quickly and in silence. Afraid we would come to my door before a word was said, I struggled to keep up with him, desperately trying to think of what to say.

Finally, at the playground he slowed his pace and moved toward the swings. Looking around, I remembered that morning, seemingly long ago, when he had found me on the bench reading aloud to myself.

When we were settled in the swings, he spoke. "It's not easy to tell about. They call what I have schizophre-

nia. Number one is"—he stopped and held up one finger—"I don't want you feeling sorry for me. And
next—" He added another finger. "I hope you
won't"—he stopped and shrugged his shoulders—"you
know. I don't want you to feel funny around me."

"I won't," I said, unsure about the truth of my
words. I gave myself a small push with my foot. He took
a big breath, and I could tell he was going to do the
talking for a while. I made my swing go just a little
higher.

"I hear voices," he said. "And sometimes I can see
the speaker just for a minute."

"Voices?"

"Well, really I should say, a voice. It's a boy. He
lived back in the 1800s, and he knew Brahms."

"Brahms?"

"The composer. You know, 'Brahms's Lullaby.'"
He hummed a little bit. "He wrote lots of other things
too. Friedrich would have been a famous composer too,
but he died young." Ethan's voice slowed with emotion,
and his eyes looked sad. I could see that this Friedrich
was a real person to Ethan.

"So this voice, do you just sort of feel it talking to
you?" I tried to believe he might mean something like

the conversations I sometimes hold with myself in my head.

Ethan sat still looking at his open hands. "No. I don't feel it or think it. I hear his voice." He told me then about how Friedrich came to him the year he was six. "My sister had just died. We lived in a camp sort of like this. Ruthie and I went out and played in the pipe yard even though we had been told not to. She was five, a year younger than me. The pipes started to roll. I got away, but she didn't."

"Oh, Ethan, how terrible for you. Do you remember it well?" I slowed my swing.

"Like it happened yesterday." He closed his eyes for a minute and ran his fingers through his hair. "Mama and I stayed with her mother on the farm for several months. She spent so much time crying. One doctor says maybe that's why I invented Friedrich."

"Like an imaginary playmate?" I asked.

He shook his head. "No, they don't put you in a mental hospital for having an imaginary playmate. Another doctor says schizophrenia has nothing to do with what happens to you. He believes they'll prove soon that the whole thing is caused by chemical problems in the brain."

He looked at me like it was my turn to talk, so I asked, "How did it start? You know when you first started seeing this Friedrich?"

"I can tell you about it exactly. I've gone over and over it in my mind for years. I found him sitting on the old piano bench at Grandma's, and I told him his clothes looked funny.

" 'It's unlikely you've ever known anyone from my country,' he answered. He laughed, and he ruffled my hair. He was really nice to me in those days."

"Did you actually think you heard his voice?" I looked down at my shoes.

Ethan nodded. "I know the exact sound of his accent. I asked him where he came from. He told me later, but that first day he said it wasn't important. He wanted to know if I wanted to be his friend. Of course, I did. I told him about Ruthie, and he understood how sad I was." Ethan paused a minute, but when I didn't say anything, he went on.

"I remember asking if he was a teenager and if he could drive a car. He told me he did not use the word teenager, but that I could think of him as sixteen. He said he couldn't drive a car, but that he could play the piano. He said pianos were much more important than cars. He played for me, and he promised to teach me to play."

"Did you tell your folks?" I asked.

Ethan shook his head. "Friedrich made me promise not to. It wasn't hard to keep the secret. My grandmother was outside most of the time, and my mother stayed in her room either crying or asleep. I quit coasting down the hill in the backyard in my little red wagon. I didn't go out to the barn to play with the kittens either, but the main thing is that I quit standing beside my mother's closed door, hoping she would come out. I loved playing the piano even though my feet wouldn't touch the floor."

"I bet you were cute," I said. Then I felt embarrassed. "That was a stupid thing to say."

Ethan didn't even seem to hear me. He left his swing and went to lean against one of the pipes that held them.

"Clare," he said very slowly. "There's something I can't understand."

There was a whole bunch I couldn't understand, but I didn't say so. "What?" I asked. "Tell me."

"Well, I was six. I knew about cowboys and about Mickey Mouse. I didn't know about composers. I had never heard of Brahms. I had no idea what a concerto was."

"What *is* a concerto? I mean, I know it's music, but I don't know what the word means."

"A piece featuring one solo instrument at a time. Friedrich wrote a piece called *Forest Concerto*, but he never got to play it in public because he died. He taught me to play so I could do it for him, but Clare, don't you see? If I made Friedrich up in my mind, where did all that information come from? How did I really learn to play the piano?"

My hands were wrapped around the swing chains hard, fingernails cutting into my palms. "That's right!" My breath came quickly. "How could a six-year-old know that stuff? Where would you even get a name like Friedrich?"

He came back to drop into his swing. "They say I must have heard it all somewhere, stored it away in my subconscious mind, but I don't know."

"You think you might not have been sick at all?" I started to hope. "You think this Friedrich might have really come to you?"

"It's not possible, is it? But how did I learn to play

that piano? I remember the scales he had me do over and over. He would skip days sometimes, and I would be so lonely. I'd sit by the big window and wait. For years I kept my promise not to tell anyone that he came. I kept it until the recital." Ethan stopped talking and stared again at his hands, moving one finger at a time like he wanted to check their mobility.

"What happened? What made them put you in the hospital?"

"My recital was a big deal in Dallas. My teacher set it up because he was so impressed with my music. Friedrich got really excited. His concerto is extremely hard to play, but he said I could do it." He was quiet, like maybe he'd forgotten I was there.

"Ethan," I said finally, "Did you do it? Did you play the *Forest Concerto*?"

"Yes. The audience loved it, clapped and clapped. They stood up, some even shouted."

"So what went wrong?"

"I saw him there. Friedrich stood in the aisle right beside the front row. He was clapping too, and he was crying, big tears rolled down his cheeks. I couldn't stand it, his never having that applause for himself. So I walked to the microphone, and I told them about the composer.

I said he was present. That part I hadn't planned to say, but it slipped out. When the recital ended, my teacher waited backstage. He wanted to know what I was talking about. I told him the whole story, how Friedrich had taught me to play and how I saw him there in the audience. He told my parents."

His blue eyes clouded with pain. I hated making him tell it all, but I had to know. "Go on," I said.

"The next thing I knew, I was in a mental hospital. They used shock treatments on me." He reached up to touch his head. I moved to stand near him, wishing I could have been near him then, wishing I could have held his hand. "They put electricity into my brain and made me have convulsions."

"Oh, no." I bit at my lip.

He shrugged. "I guess it wasn't so bad. I wasn't conscious." He shook his head, "But I hated knowing what they did. I hated it so much."

I hated it too. I put my hand out to touch his shoulder.

He looked up at me, and what he said next was the worst part. "It's not over, Clare. Please don't tell anyone, but it's not over. Friedrich has come to me since we moved here. He's angry because I've forgotten his piece.

He helped me play it, those nights you heard. He wants me to write it down."

"Ethan," I said, and I could feel the tears slipping from my eyes. "Oh, Ethan."

"I don't want to go back to that hospital," he said. "I want to live here and go to school with you." He paused and looked down at his feet. "I think maybe I would rather be dead than go back to being hooked to those machines."

SEVEN

The carefree days with Ethan were gone. The knowledge of his illness sat on my shoulders like a great dark cloak that I couldn't take off. For a minute, I might forget about having it on, but if I tried to run through the grass, the cloak would trip me up.

We did not talk about Friedrich or about the possibility that Ethan would go back to the hospital. We laughed and had fun, but the question stood always between us. A couple of times I had to whisper, "Have you heard him?" Ethan shook his head, and I squeezed his hand, hoping.

The start of school got close, and it helped to get our mind off things a little. Just a few days after Ethan's revelation, I received Motie Ann's annual phone call, a sure sign that school would start soon. She wanted just to confirm that we were still friends, that I would be there to smile at her in the halls. Motie Ann was too shy to come around much when I was with other people, and I usually didn't get around to spending much time with her. Still she considered me her best, her only friend.

Sometimes, because she liked having papers to hand in, I would help Motie Ann with an assignment. The teachers, who expected nothing from her, were kind to her.

In high school mostly only a few cruel boys teased her, but that had not always been true. It was because I joined those who hurt Motie Ann in third grade that we got to be friends and I learned to appreciate her real goodness.

"Motie Ann's got dumb germs," someone would say. "If she touches you, you'll get 'em."

She did, in those days, look sort of germ-ridden. Mr. Rawlings had recently died after a long illness. Motie Ann and her mother continued to live on the family farm, but Mrs. Rawlings, whose other six children were already away from home, seemed just too tired to take interest in keeping up appearances for herself or her little retarded daughter. Motie Ann came dirty and bewildered each day to school, where she was met with jeers and ridicule.

At Christmas, like always, our class drew names for a gift exchange. Everyone hoped to get the name of someone they especially liked, and much secrecy surrounded the drawing.

"Motie Ann's got yours," the girl who sat behind me whispered. "I bet you don't get a thing."

"I bet she can't even read whose name it is," another girl said.

"Who would want anything Motie Ann brought anyhow?" I said.

The Christmas party lost all appeal for me. Either I would be left with nothing when the presents got passed out, or I would be watched by everyone as I opened some detestable gift.

"I don't feel good," I told my mother on the morning of the party. It was true. My stomach cramped with agitation.

My closet held a new red taffeta dress, finished by my mother only the night before. Nothing less than a fever would have prevented Mom's zipping me into that dress and sending me off to have a wonderful time.

"It's just the excitement," Mom said. "You'll feel better when you get to school."

She was wrong. The party was scheduled for two o'clock, and I felt worse and worse as the time drew closer. At the back of the room sat a Christmas tree decorated with our construction paper chains and with Mrs. Kemp's bright glass bulbs. Under the tree, we had stacked gifts. One of them read, "To Clare from Motie Ann," in what must have been her mother's printing. When I saw it, I knew I would have preferred receiving no gift at all.

The teacher chose Nancy Potter to pass out the gifts. Catching the droopy bow between thumb and finger, she delivered the dreaded package to me, who believed everyone stared.

"It's germy," Nancy Potter whispered from behind me. "It's got Motie germs."

I sat for a while thinking of pretending to throw up. I considered putting my hand over my mouth, making a sort of gagging sound, and running from the room. In third grade, however, I believed the truth could be easily observed by adults. Mrs. Kemp, no doubt, would know that I faked being sick. Dragging me back, the teacher would hand me the present and demand that I open it there at the front of the room.

Somehow I got the paper off and opened the box, which contained a small bottle. "Rose Toilet Water," the label said. Nancy leaned over my shoulder. "It's water from Motie Ann's toilet." She laughed.

I had seen the product in the Edmond variety store and knew that toilet water was an old-fashioned word for cologne. I knew that what Nancy said was meant to be funny. Still, I felt suddenly that I might not have to pretend the vomiting scene.

Finally the party ended and the bell rang, signaling the end of the school day. I gathered my things, slowly, hoping to be the last one out and so escape any more comments on my gift. The problem was Nancy, living just down from the school, did not ride a bus. She took forever to leave her desk.

I was almost out of the room when Nancy called. "Hey, what's that smell? You put on some of Motie's toilet water?"

The wastebasket stood by the door. Mrs. Kemp was outside on bus duty. I drew back and threw the bottle into the can as hard as possible. Then I looked up. Motie

Ann stood in the door. Her eyes were big and round and filled up with misery. Her lips were pressed hard against her teeth, and her hand shot up to them, like to hold back a scream.

All during the long Christmas vacation I wrestled with the memory of how Motie Ann looked. When school opened again, I waited outside for her bus.

"I'll walk in with you," I told her.

Motie Ann beamed. The gift, it seemed, was either forgotten or unimportant when compared with an offer of friendship.

And so we became school friends, and Motie Ann, probably with the help of her mother, called me each fall.

"Have you bought your school clothes?" I asked her when the phone call came. Somewhere in the past Mrs. Rawlings had mustered her strength, and her daughter had begun coming to school clean and better dressed. The year before, I had been asked to go with them to Edmond and had helped select three dresses that I thought sort of flattered Motie Ann.

"Naw," she said. "I ain't going to buy none. Might be I won't go to school so long this year."

"Oh," I said. "You shouldn't drop out." Immediately I wondered about the statement. What could school do for Motie Ann? We had no special classes to help her.

"I might get me a job," she said.

That, of course, was impossible. There would never be a job for Motie Ann. After her mother's death, what would become of her?

"Don't make up your mind right now," I told her. "Let's talk to Mr. Elliot. Maybe he will have some ideas for you." By the time we hung up, Motie Ann had agreed to start back to school.

That afternoon I told Ethan about Motie Ann. We sat on my front porch, and we dripped water from our clothes. Ethan had just pushed me into the spray from the front-yard sprinkler. I pulled him in after me, and we both ended up soaked and cool. When the laughing died down, I started explaining about Motie Ann.

"When can I meet her?" he asked.

"Well," I said, "I hardly see her except at school." Suddenly I felt sort of bad about that.

Ethan squeezed some water from his T-shirt. "I lived next to a kid like Motie Ann in Dallas. He couldn't read or stuff, but he could tell you what day of the week any date in the past fell on."

"How could he do that?" I asked.

Ethan shrugged. "I don't know, but in lots of ways he was pretty regular. I guess on the inside people are mostly alike."

Water drained from my hair and ran down my forehead toward my eyes. I reached up to wipe at it, but Ethan's hand got there first. His fingers touched my skin, and I had to make myself breathe normally. I forgot all about Motie Ann.

Just then Teddy came bursting out the door. "Wow, you two been kissing or something?" he shouted.

I reached out to grab at Teddy's leg, but he jumped off the porch to get away from me and went out into the yard to run through the sprinkler. I felt embarrassed and wanted to think of something to say to Ethan.

"Do you miss your friends in Dallas?" I asked.

He nodded, "Yeah. Well, really just one."

"A girl, I bet," I said, and then I was embarrassed again.

"Are you asking if I have a girlfriend?" he said without looking at me. He took off one shoe and emptied water from it.

"Well, do you?" I tried real hard to make my voice sound easy, like the answer didn't matter all that much.

"The friend I mentioned is a boy, but there is a girl I care a lot about." I wanted to go through the porch and into the ground, but he went on. "She's not in Dallas. She's right here beside me. Her folks might think she's too young to have a real boyfriend, but that doesn't change how I feel about her."

I didn't say anything, just reached out and touched his hand. He wrapped his fingers around mine. A couple of other little kids had come up to run through the water with Teddy. They laughed and shouted at each other. To me their voices sounded beautiful.

EIGHT

A few days later two important things happened. For the first time in two months it rained, not a big thunder-and-lightning thing like we have in the spring, just rain, steady and warm. Almost everyone in the camp went outside.

The men down in the pipe yard stopped unloading their trucks, took off their steel hats, and let the rain fall on their heads. Women didn't even run for the clothes that hung on their lines. They just stood on their porches and laughed.

Ethan and I made mud pies. We sat in my backyard, soaking wet, and made wonderful pastries of mud. We were in the middle of a contest to see whose creations were best when the second thing happened. Liz came home.

I had just stacked a three-tiered creation in front of Ethan. "I can do better than that," he said. He plunged his hands into the mud and began to roll a big glob between his fingers.

That's when Liz appeared. I jumped up, surprised to see her and surprised by how glad I was to see her. Liz hadn't been on my mind much.

Liz stepped back. "You can hug me later," she said, and she laughed.

I shook the mud from my hands. "Gosh, I'm glad you're home."

We talked for a few minutes about how Liz's aunt was doing fine now. "Go home and change your clothes," I suggested. "You can help us."

"No, I've got to unpack," Liz said. She looked back once to wave. I knew I should have gone with her, but I just didn't want to.

"I'll come over right after supper," I called to her as she walked away. I guess maybe that's when I chose between Liz and Ethan. No, I had made the choice long before.

Later at Liz's house we discussed school's starting and who our teachers would be. While Liz took clothes from the suitcase, I walked around the room. On the dresser sat a framed picture of the two of us dressed in hobo jeans with patches and bundles on sticks over our shoulders. Our smiles showed front teeth that we had blacked out with licorice.

I remembered how we had laughed, almost choking on the candy. I wanted to think of something we could giggle about now. It seemed like a long time since I had laughed with Liz. I stood by her record player, pushing the turntable with my finger.

"You didn't write me very often," she said from the other side of the room. "I kept wanting you to tell me more about Ethan."

"Sorry about the letters." I shrugged and decided to tell the truth. "I guess I've been all caught up in getting to know him."

Liz grinned, lifted her suitcase off to the floor, and stretched across the bed. "So. Tell. I want to know details right now."

Suddenly, I did want to talk. More than anything, I wanted to tell Liz all about my summer days with Ethan. "He's so special," I said, and I went over to sit beside her. "And he likes me. He really, really does. We've had lots of fun together, just hanging around here. He makes everything exciting." I looked at Liz and waited for a response.

"Gosh, that's great." She got up and started taking things from the suitcase again. "So you two are a couple, like all the ones at school?"

"No." I stood up too. This was important. There was so much more between Ethan and me than there was between the couples at school who just wanted to hang all over each other every chance they got. "It's not just touching and stuff. Shoot, it's hard to explain. I guess Ethan makes me want to be a better person, and he tells me all about his problems." I was sorry as soon as I said that last part, but it was too late.

"Problems?" Liz studied me real close. "What problems?"

"Oh, you know. He's awful serious about his music, and I guess his folks want him to get involved in other things more."

She didn't say anything for a second. "There's more, Clare. You're not telling me everything, are you?"

"I am. Don't I always?"

"You used to." There was a great big white silence

in the room between us. I could feel Liz starting to get mad, but then she forced a little laugh. "It's no big deal." She laid the last piece from her suitcase on a chair. "Boy, do I ever have to work to get ready for my recital."

"You can do it though," I said, glad to have a change of subject.

"I guess. You still want to go? To the recital, I mean?" She had a hanger in her hand and a dress, but she just held them, waiting. "It's the first Saturday after school starts, and I'll have to tell them how many tickets I need."

"Sure." I nodded. "I've had it marked on the kitchen calendar for ages."

"Okay, then." Liz smiled. "I'm glad you still want to."

We tried to talk some more, but that big white silence thing never did leave the room. Liz told me about things her little cousin said, but we didn't laugh even once. I didn't stay too long.

Later, I wandered home through the evening that still dripped rain. "Everything's just wet," I said aloud, but I felt real sad. I couldn't be sure if the dampness around my eyes came from rain or tears.

NINE

Just two days after Liz came home, school started. January first never feels like the beginning of a year to me, but the start of a school term does. Once there had been new crayons and Big Chief tablets to mark the fresh start. Now I bought spiral notebooks and ballpoint pens to signal that I would soon be a sophomore in high school. Writing my name on the new notebooks, I tried hard to think only good thoughts.

I had kept a careful eye on Ethan and saw no sign of illness or of a boy who had strange visitors from the past. He would not, I decided, ever be ill again. It wouldn't happen. I knew it wouldn't because I could not bear to watch.

On that last evening of summer vacation, Liz came

over to my house. "I wanted to show you my new outfit," she said, holding out a hanger with a navy pleated
skirt and a red blouse on it.

We went into my room to talk and listen to the
radio. Later we popped some corn and ate it, lying on
our backs with our feet resting on my bed. "Let's not say
anything funny," Liz suggested. "We could get choked
on this popcorn and die."

"Yeah, let's don't talk about the time Mrs. Pulley
came out of the faculty rest room between classes and
walked all the way down the hall with her dress tail
caught up in her girdle," I said.

We did laugh then, and it felt good, especially since
neither of us choked. I went out on the porch with Liz
when it was time for her to go. "Come walk home with
me," she said.

I hesitated. We'd had a good time and had not mentioned Ethan even once. I knew he would probably be
practicing. I didn't want to stand in the road with Liz,
listen to Ethan's music, and wonder if Friedrich was there
beside him. Liz would be too likely to pick up on my
distress.

"Come on," she said again, and I followed her down
the steps.

Sure enough, we started hearing music before too long. Dark had almost settled on the camp, which seemed quieter than usual. I imagined that everyone had open windows, and we were all listening to our special camp musician.

Liz, though, paid no attention to the music. She rattled on about how she dreaded biology class because of the dissecting we would have to do. "Don't you agree with me?" she asked.

"Huh?"

"I said that I think it's wrong to cut up frogs." Liz sounded sort of aggravated, but I wasn't sure if she was put out with me or with the guys who killed the frogs and put them in formaldehyde.

"I guess frogs have to be sacrificed for science. Who knows, one of our illustrious classmates may become a brain surgeon or something," I said. "But anyway, I'd better go." I started to back away, still listening to the music. Ethan had changed pieces, and I was pretty certain that the notes I heard came from Friedrich's concerto.

"See you in the morning at the bus," Liz called.

Now I had two problems to think about as I trudged home, kicking the gravel in front of me. Liz and I had been riding that bus together for nine years. We always got on together, and we always sat together. In the morning, of course, I'd sit with Ethan. It shouldn't be a big deal, but I had a feeling Liz might not agree.

The next morning I took my time walking down to the gate, even though Teddy yelled, "You'd better run. Here it comes."

I wanted to get there just in time to get on, not in time to stand with Liz, Ethan, and the others who waited.

"Hurry," Ethan shouted, and he stepped back to wait for me while the others got ready to get on.

I did run then, keeping my eyes on Ethan's dark hair and smiling face. A familiar television commercial flashed through my mind. There was music, and a girl ran through a field into a boy's arms. I would run to Ethan, run to sit beside him on the bus, no matter whose feelings it hurt.

We eased into a seat near the front. I spotted a place right across from us, but Liz moved on toward the back. "Liz," I called, "There's a seat up here." I wasn't sure if she heard me or not, because she pushed her way through to a seat in the very back.

"Are you okay?" I searched Ethan's face for any sign of strain.

He smiled. "Sure. Excited about my first day." We

were crowded into a seat with a little kid, so our shoulders touched. It was the best ride I'd ever had on that bus.

When we lurched to a stop, Ethan and I got off almost first. He had to go into the office to complete his enrollment. "I'll wait for Liz," I told him. "We're not supposed to be in the building until just before the bell rings."

"Gosh, you waited for me," Liz said when she got off.

I decided to ignore the sarcastic tone. I'd be patient and careful not to let her feel left out.

A group of junior and senior girls were standing near the big doors. Liz and I didn't join them, but we walked up the steps to stand and could hear what they said.

"There's that old goat, Elliot. I was hoping he would expire over the summer," Judy Preston said.

Liz and I turned to watch Mr. Elliot, bald, odd, and somewhat unaware of the world outside of books, get out of his car. In the past I had kept my favorable opinion to myself.

"Don't worry. His days are numbered." Imogene Whitaker finished putting on her lipstick before saying more. The group waited. Imogene's father was president of the school board. "Daddy says he won't be offered a contract in the spring."

"Probably cry like he does when he recites that stuff about the quality of mercy," Judy said. She leaned against Imogene's shoulder, and they giggled.

When I turned back, Ethan had just come out. I caught his eye and saw that he had heard the comments. Ethan knew how I felt about Mr. Elliot, and I could feel him waiting for me to say something. "He's the best teacher we have," I said, and I waved at the man who got out of his car.

Liz spoke up then. "That's right," she said.

I was surprised to hear some murmurs of agreement, and several others waved at Mr. Elliot. I made up my mind to start way before spring contract time to get up support for my favorite teacher. Liz and Ethan would help me. I smiled at them. We'd have a good year, the three of us together.

Ethan made everything different at school. I could just feel how excited the girls all were over having a handsome new boy in school, but it was me he waited for between every class. Remembering to include Liz took a lot of energy. I made a point to save her a seat in history class that first morning, but things didn't work as well as I had hoped. Even though we sat near each other in every class, things had changed. The two-girls-against-the-world feeling had disappeared.

That first Monday Liz went with Ethan and me to Griffith's for a hamburger at lunch, but there were only two empty seats together at the counter. Liz slid into a single one near the door. "We'll ask someone to trade with you," I said, but Liz shook her head. Ethan and I got busy talking and had hardly begun our burgers when Liz finished hers and slipped out.

I decided right there at lunch that I would make time in the evening to go over to Liz's or get her to come over to my house. We'd have lots of things to talk about after our first day of school. In all my afternoon classes, I made little notes about things I had noticed that Liz and I could laugh about. I had a whole page of things like, "Rosemary Williams either grew a bunch this summer or she's been stuffing her bra again. We'll know if the tissue works out and sticks out the arm hole of her sleeveless dress like it did last spring."

It made me feel good and loyal to plan for time with

Liz. When Ethan and I got off the bus, I told him to walk on ahead. "I need to say something to Liz," I said. "I'll catch up with you."

"Hey, there you are," Liz said when she stepped down. "I didn't imagine I'd see anything except your back." She pointed with her head toward Ethan, who was walking ahead of us. "Run on and be with him. It's okay."

I shook my head. "Don't go getting all worked up. I was thinking that after supper tonight you might want to come over. We didn't get much of a chance to talk today."

She looked at me for a second like she might not believe me, but then she smiled. "Sure," she said. "Right after supper." Then she surprised me by yelling, "Hey, Ethan, wait for us."

I should have just let it go at that, but I got carried away with my planning to be loyal. "Why don't we plan to spend every Monday evening together?" I said. "Just us girls."

Liz shifted her books from one arm to the other. "So I need an appointment now to see you, like you're a doctor or something." She shook her head hard enough to throw her blond hair out behind her. "Never mind, Clare. Just work me in whenever you get an opening." She walked on and passed Ethan, who was waiting for me.

That night Liz called me. "I'm sorry," she said. "I know I acted like an idiot."

"It's all right," I told her. I had a flashback to July, when Liz first met Ethan. "I guess I know how you feel, but Liz, I really, really do care about Ethan, and I want you to be his friend too."

"Sure," she said, but I didn't really think it would be that easy.

We talked a few minutes more, but I didn't bring up Rosemary Williams or any of the other notes I had taken. "I've got to go practice," she said after just a minute. "Don't forget my recital on Saturday," she said just before we hung up.

I was determined to include Liz at lunch the next day, and I told Ethan I would meet him at her locker.

"Do you want to go to the store or eat in the cafeteria?" I asked her.

She was putting away her books, but she paused and looked at me. "Oh, didn't I tell you Barbara Fisher and I are going straight to the gym?"

Lockers banged everywhere, and I thought maybe I hadn't heard her right. "The gym? What about lunch?"

She took a brown paper bag from her locker. "We brought our lunch. Coach said we could eat over there and get an early start practicing our shots."

"So you planned this yesterday?"

Liz shrugged. "Well, you know Coach would never let a boy be over there with us, so of course I knew you wouldn't be interested."

I didn't look at her. It was true that I didn't want to give up eating with Ethan, but I would have liked being asked. Barbara Fisher was a girl in our class who wanted to make the main string as much as Liz and I did. I didn't think she had much of a chance, even with the extra practice, but I wondered when she and Liz had got to be such pals.

Ethan came toward me. "Okay," I said to Liz. "Guess I'll see you in gym." I hurried to meet Ethan.

Maybe Ethan made things tough with Liz, but it sure worked the other way with Motie Ann. It started the second morning of school. Ethan and I were standing off a little from everyone else, waiting for time to go in the building. Motie Ann's bus had just arrived, and she came toward us, grinning. I had been surprised the day before because Motie Ann had taken to Ethan right off, even telling him about the little nephew and niece who were visiting at her house.

On that second morning, Motie Ann looked forward to talking to Ethan more. I could tell by the way she moved in our direction. When she was only a few feet from us, two boys caught up to her from behind and said something. Melvin Erikson and his friend Jerry Bob Miller were notorious for tormenting Motie Ann.

She stopped and looked at them. The big, happy smile slipped off her lips and was replaced with a lip-biting look of pain.

"They're teasing her," I said. I dropped my books and started toward them.

Ethan reached out and caught my arm. "Wait," he said, stepping around me and heading for Motie Ann.

I opened my mouth to warn him against fighting. Mr. Harris, our principal, wouldn't tolerate fighting for any reason. No words came out, though, because Ethan had already crossed the few feet that separated us from Motie Ann and the boys.

Holding my breath, I watched. The boys had stopped talking and were staring at Ethan. Melvin's hands were forming fists, and Jerry Bob, I knew, would jump into any fight Melvin started. Not only would Ethan be beaten up, he would probably be suspended for fighting right along with the other two.

It didn't work out that way. Ethan didn't speak to the boys at all. "Motie Ann," I heard him say. "Clare and I have been waiting for you." He held out his hand.

Motie Ann's face brightened. With her head held high, she took Ethan's hand and walked beside him back to where I stood. I had never really noticed before what a beautiful smile Motie Ann had.

Melvin and Jerry Bob stood there with stupid looks on their faces.

TEN

There were things about that first week of school that I should have done differently, things I should have been smarter about. Maybe it was being away from the camp, where my father or mother could come up behind us at any minute, but Ethan and I started being more physical, holding hands a lot. Every time he took my hand, I hated that it would be almost another year before we could go on a real date. I admit that by Friday, I wasn't thinking about much except Ethan.

That day almost everyone ate in the cafeteria because on Fridays the cooks made huge, sticky, sweet cinnamon rolls for dessert. I looked around for Liz, but I guess she and Barbara thought basketball was more important than cinnamon rolls.

Ethan, Motie Ann, and I ate with some other kids. When Ethan headed for that table, I started to protest on account of Motie Ann. I thought sure she would turn away and find a spot by herself because she never liked being around a group. Ethan sat down first. I saw Motie Ann hesitate, glance at an empty table a few feet away, then move on to sit across from Ethan. For just a second tears came to my eyes when I realized how much Ethan had changed Motie Ann's life in just five days. She felt safe across from him.

Andy Crews and John Bingham were talking about a car they were working on. "Will you take me for a ride?" asked Doris Eakins.

"Sure. We may get her going tonight." Cars were his passion, and Andy waved his fork as he talked. He turned to Ethan. "What kind of wheels do you have?"

Uneasy, I fingered the hem of my blouse sleeve and stared at Ethan, who seemed perfectly comfortable. He licked at the icing that had come off his roll onto his fingers. "Don't have a car, but every once in a while I get my hands on my dad's '58 Ford."

I studied my cinnamon bun carefully. "Every once in a while." What an exaggeration, but I supposed Ethan was allowed a little of what most boys seemed to do all the time.

His next words were even more unexpected. "By the way, Clare, I've got the car tomorrow. Want to go to Oklahoma City?"

"Sounds good." I hoped to leave it at that, but Doris, well aware of my father's rule, stared at me.

"Well, I mean, I'll try to get Dad to say okay."

"Good," said Ethan. He began to tackle his roll happily, as if he hadn't just been spouting hot air.

I ate slowly, hoping the others would finish and leave the table. When the last boy threw his leg over the bench to go, I spoke. "You just want those guys to think you drive and everything, I guess." It was natural, I thought, for him to have trouble at times enduring it all.

"No." He shook his head earnestly. "They've cut my medicine. It's my maiden voyage." He looked at me over his milk carton. "You aren't afraid to ride with me, are you?"

"You know I'm not."

"Ethan's your boyfriend," Motie Ann said to me, and I nodded. It was a fact, and I would do whatever I had to to go with him on Saturday.

"Next time we go somewhere, how about if you go with us?" Ethan said to Motie Ann. They started talking about places we might go. I didn't even try to follow their conversation. My mind raced to make lists of things to say to my dad.

Gym came after lunch. By the time I had dressed for practice, I had given up any hope. My father wouldn't change his mind, ever.

I was on the court playing when I made my decision. The ball was at the other end of the court. "Okay," I said, half aloud, and I stomped my tennis shoe hard against the court. "If I can't reason with him, I'll lie."

At supper I staged my performance. "Oh, Mom," I said, and I looked right at her. "I forgot to tell you, Motie Ann wants me to go with her to Edmond tomorrow for shopping."

Mom liked my kindness to Motie Ann. "So," she said smiling, "she changed her mind." I had told her about the phone conversation.

"Yeah, we're leaving right after breakfast, make a day of it. Maybe go to a movie later. Okay?"

"Certainly." She reached over and squeezed my hand. "I see some very good things in you, honey." I tried to smile back in spite of the pain in my stomach.

A day with Ethan, alone, driving free, eating out and everything! It would be the most exciting day of my life. The last day, more than likely, if my parents found out. All evening I turned the pages of a magazine while I struggled to sit still and watch television with the family.

When Liz called, I was glad for the distraction. At least I was glad until I heard what she had to say.

She started the conversation with, "Boy, I hardly saw you at school all week."

It was quite an exaggeration. I'd seen her in every class, but I knew what she meant. Still, I didn't feel too guilty. Hadn't I planned to work at not leaving her out? She was the one who had broken away and made lunch plans without me.

"Guess we were both pretty busy," I said.

The bombshell came next. "You haven't forgotten about my recital?" she asked.

"No," I barely got the word out. My throat filled up, and my heart pounded. "Tell me again what time."

"We'll leave at ten," she said. "After it's over, we'll go out to eat. Be home by two or three."

"It's marked on the kitchen calendar," I said, and there it was, "L's recital," plain as day. But I had not looked at the calendar lately, had not thought about Liz's big day since Monday.

Ten till two or three. There would be no way to go with Liz and with Ethan. I should have hung up and called Ethan to say I couldn't go with him. After all, I had promised Liz long before I even knew him. At the very least I should have told Liz right out that I wouldn't be going. I didn't do either one.

I hung up, half choking on my good-bye, and sat staring at the phone. The easiest thing to do would be to just go. Liz would call my house and hear that I had gone off with Motie Ann. She would be hurt. No, she would be furious, but she would get over it. I told myself I had no choice. I belonged beside Ethan.

In bed, too full of anticipation and guilt for much sleep, I lay awake watching the moon through my window and listening to the oil pump.

When morning finally came, I threw most of my pancakes in the trash and poured my milk down the drain. "I'm going to walk down to the main gate to wait for them," I called to my mother, who had started her Saturday cleaning of the bathroom.

Outside I kicked at the gravel on the road and told myself that my parents had no communication with Mrs.

Rawlings. They would never know, and I would have one special golden day to remember. Still, I looked back over my shoulder. No, Mom, toilet brush in hand, did not pursue me. It was hard not to run madly down the road.

"I would have picked you up," Ethan said when he answered my knock. He told me his parents had gone to Tulsa in the Ford. "We'll have to take the Rambler," he said.

I couldn't have cared less what car we drove. When we got to the car, he opened the door for me, and I knew this was a real date. I felt like singing with happiness. It was while Ethan walked to his side of the car that I glanced up to see Liz standing on her front porch. She had on her ballet outfit. Her face twisted, like she might cry.

"I should get out of this car," I whispered to myself, and I shifted on the seat. "I'll get out, tell Ethan I can't go, call off the date." I reached for the door handle, but I didn't grip it.

Ethan got in. "All set?" He settled behind the wheel and turned the key. No words came out of my mouth. I smiled at him, but turned back to see Liz go inside. I thought of Motie Ann's face as I smashed her Christmas present. Liz wouldn't be so quick to forgive. Would she still call my house? Would she tell my parents that I had gone off with Ethan?

At first Ethan kept his lips pressed tight against his teeth, his eyes strictly on the road ahead, his hands gripping the wheel hard. I looked out the window. For this I lied to my parents and betrayed my closest friend.

Gradually, though, he relaxed, smiling at me and talking about things along the road. I tried to push my lie and the look on Liz's face out of my mind.

"Want to go to the zoo?" he asked.

I didn't. It was too childish a thing to do on such an important day, but I just shrugged. "Sure, I always like to see Judy." I told Ethan about how kids all over Oklahoma had taken pennies to school to buy the elephant for the Oklahoma City Zoo.

"I think in Texas we grew our own elephants out on the range," he said, and I laughed.

I shouldn't have worried about the zoo being a waste. Strolling through the grounds with Ethan wasn't anything like going with my family or my fourth-grade class. There were lots of young couples, some obviously in love.

At the polar bear's cage Ethan put his arms around

me. "Poor guy," he said, pointing to the animal. "He's all alone." I leaned against him and wanted to stay there forever. Being in Ethan's arms, I thought, was worth any amount of wrath from Liz or even from my parents. After a while we moved on, holding hands.

Peacocks roamed the zoo grounds freely, and their cries provided a strange but appealing background music. Ethan spotted a fallen peacock feather and picked it up. Bowing deeply, he handed it to me. "For my lady," he said like a knight.

That's what Ethan was, a knight, gentle and kind, but ready to defend the right. He had experienced lots of pain, but the suffering had made him strong. As we strolled around the zoo grounds that sunny day, I believed our days together were just beginning. I carried the peacock feather carefully and thought it would be the first of many mementos.

After the zoo, we went to Beverly's Chicken in the Rough. "I could see a place sort of like this from my hospital window in Dallas," Ethan told me. "When things got rough, I used to imagine I was in that restaurant with a pretty girl." He squeezed my hand. "Now it's come true."

Walking in beside him, I did feel pretty, and the

rather ordinary eating place was elegant because across from me sat a boy whose special smile flashed in my direction.

I had done fairly well at blocking thoughts of Liz and my parents while we were at the zoo, but while we ate I kept remembering Liz's face. I had hurt her, really hurt the friend who had been beside me always. Wondering how I could ever make it up to Liz worried me even more than my parents' anger.

"Guess we'd better head back," Ethan said reluctantly when we put down the last chicken bone. I could hardly make myself nod agreement. Another such day would not come until my birthday in the spring, unless I wanted to make a habit of lying to my parents. Even if they didn't find out this time, the pain in my stomach told me I didn't want to try it again.

It was when we pulled out from the restaurant that the accident happened. I saw the truck barreling down Twenty-third Street, heard the screeching of the tires, and knew that it would hit us. But there was no time to scream or even turn my head away before the impact left our car whirling in the street.

When the spinning stopped, I heard myself scream. "Ethan! Ethan!"

Finally I became aware that he too was yelling. "Are you hurt? Clare, are you okay?"

There was a cut on Ethan's forehead, probably from being thrown into the steering wheel. My right shoulder and arm throbbed from impact with the dashboard.

The truck had hit us on Ethan's side, but in the back. A couple of feet to the front, and Ethan would have had a lot more than a cut on the forehead. I started to shake all over.

Even before we had climbed from the damaged car, the full meaning of the accident hit me. Our parents would have to be called!

"Don't worry," the policeman told Ethan after he had looked us over. "That fellow will have to take care of your car." He wrote information on his pad. "No doubt about it. He went right through that light, speeding too." He pointed to Ethan's car. "You kids can't drive that job for a while. Go get in the squad. We'll call your folks from the station. You're going to be bruised and sore tomorrow, but you're lucky. If he had got you in the front, we'd be taking you out on stretchers."

I stared at the policeman. I examined my arms and felt my head, longing for a broken arm or maybe a skull fracture. Probably under those circumstances my father would feel sorry for me.

We held hands in the backseat of the black-and-white police car. "Guess I might as well tell you," I whispered to Ethan. "My folks think I'm in Edmond with Motie Ann."

He gave me a weak smile. "Well, as my mother would say, birds of a feather flock together." He pointed to the peacock plume clasped in my other hand. "My folks think I'm home working on an English assignment."

Ethan's parents weren't home yet, so mine drove to the city for us. While we waited, Ethan sat with his head in his hands. I couldn't be still. Walking around the station and occasionally going out to cover the sidewalk, I imagined how it would be.

First my dad would have to be pulled off Ethan by the policemen. Then he would turn to me and very calmly explain that I would not leave my room until my eighteenth birthday. Even school and church would be done by correspondence.

My dire predictions did not come true, but they might have been better than what did happen. My father was deadly quiet, uttering only one phrase under his breath during Mom's loud and tearful examination of us both for injuries.

"Crazy kid," he muttered.

The reference, of course, was to me, but it was Ethan who reacted with an almost physical jerking away. Actually, I didn't see him move. The recoil was an inner one, reflected only in his eyes and expressionless face. To me it felt as if he had jumped, screaming, "Don't touch me."

"Thank God you're both safe," Mom would declare periodically, unaware of the irony of her words. As Ethan sat huddled on his side of the car, it was horribly clear to me that he was not at all safe.

After a bit, I reached out to touch his arm. He made absolutely no response. I knew that he felt no contact between us. Not only was our communication gone, Ethan himself was gone, far away. I shivered despite the hot Oklahoma sun that burned through the window.

"Oh, Clare, the agony we went through thinking you had run away." My mother's words interrupted my thoughts. I leaned toward the front seat.

"Mom," I said, patting her shoulder, "you know I wouldn't run away. Did the policeman think we had?"

"No, it was earlier, after Mrs. Rawlings called to

thank you for being such a friend to Motie Ann at school."

Mom clucked her tongue. "We were just frantic until Liz told the truth."

I wrinkled my face with confusion. "Liz told the truth?"

"Yes," Mom shook her finger at me. "Don't you be mad at her, either. We called her, of course, as soon as she got home from her recital. Clare, how could you hurt her like that, skipping her big day?" Mom shook her finger again. "I'm afraid she's more loyal than you are. She hated to tell, went in your room saying she would look for clues. I guess she just realized in there that she had to tell the truth about how you and Ethan were going to Oklahoma City for the day."

Breathing hard, I let my body fall back against the rear seat. It was the ultimate climax. Liz had read my journal.

ELEVEN

"Go to your room," Dad shouted when we stepped inside the house after dropping off Ethan. It's starting now, I thought, no more sunshine or fresh air, but it was my journal, open on my desk, that got to me more than fear of punishment. I had to talk to Liz. She just had to keep the secret. Maybe, I tortured myself, Liz has already told about Ethan's illness.

Stretched on the bed, I waited. Finally they came in. Mom sat beside me on the bed. Dad stood looking down at me, patting his foot like he was keeping time to music, as he spoke.

"Clare, I never have been disappointed in you like this before. It was awful hard on your mama."

I sat up. "I'm sorry." And, oh, I was. Because of

my lie, Liz knew all about Ethan's illness. No punishment from my father could be so harsh.

"That fool that hit you needs locking up." He shook his head slowly. "Still, you did break a rule. You lied to us. That's the worst part."

I hadn't cried at all until then. "I'm sorry. I'll never do it again," I told him. Silently I pleaded with God. If Liz just hasn't blabbed, I'll never lie again, not to anyone.

"Don't cry." Mom moved to put an arm around me. "No real harm's been done."

"Oh, yes." I couldn't quit sobbing. "There is a bunch of harm that's been done." I tried to force the picture of Ethan's trancelike expression from my mind.

"Now, Clare," Dad's voice was softer than before. "This is how it is. There won't be any big punishment, but you're going to be spending Saturdays here in the house for a while. Your mother will leave some of the cleaning for you. You won't be going over to Liz's even. And if anything like this was to ever happen again . . . if it does, the rule about no dating until you're sixteen goes out the window. It'll be none until after high school."

I wiped my eyes and stared unbelieving. Staying home on Saturdays to clean. It was nothing compared to what I'd expected, but my bigger problems still loomed large. Mom gave me a hug, and Dad patted my head before they left. I made myself sit still until they closed the door. Then rushing to the bathroom, I washed my face.

"Can I go to Liz's? I need to apologize to her." My folks were in the living room watching the evening news on television. I thought of vowing not to set foot in a car, but decided to let it rest.

"Supper's in an hour," Mom said. "I was just about to put the stew on when we got the call."

Now I could add a late supper to my list of sins. "You get right back here, young lady," my father said.

On the way I stopped for a few minutes at the swings. Some kids played in the sandbox, but they didn't come over to me. I wanted to plan very carefully what to say to Liz, but for a minute I just sat there listening to the oil pump and to the Saturday evening sounds of the camp.

Someone slammed a car door, probably unloading sacks of groceries brought from Edmond. Most suppers were over, and the kids had just a little more time to play before dark. Pretty soon I'd hear calls for the sand builders' baths and weekly shampoos. Practically every kid in the camp greeted Sunday morning with squeaky clean hair. I touched my own hair, damp from perspiration. I wished shampoo could wash away my troubles.

Liz knew about Ethan's illness, and I had to be careful. We used to play set-the-table on the teeter-totter, balancing some object between us. We had to stay exactly the same distance from the ground. It required skill, and so would this balancing act. I took a deep breath and started toward Liz's, leaving the empty swing behind.

Mrs. Teal let me in. "Liz is in her room," she said. Her voice was cool, and I looked down at the living room floor. Of course Mrs. Teal wouldn't like the way I had hurt Liz. Well, there was no time to fret over that now. Without waiting for more conversation, I headed for the hall.

Liz's sister Linda was in their room too. She had paper dolls spread out on her bed. With one look at my face, she gathered her things quickly and left. Liz never glanced up at me.

"Please." I was about to cry, and I didn't try to hide the sound in my voice. The thought came to me that maybe if I cried, Liz would feel sorry for me like my parents had.

She got up and slammed the door Linda had left open. I didn't see any sign of sympathy in the slam.

"You read my journal." Too much like an accusation, I told myself, so I added, "Of course, I know you had to do it."

Liz folded her arms in front of her body and stared at me without saying a word. Get right at it, I decided. "Liz, please promise me you won't say anything about Ethan. About him being sick and all. It's all just a big mistake anyway. The doctors didn't understand. That's all."

Liz made a little snorting sound. "They don't lock people in mental hospitals for nothing." She turned back toward the door like the conversation was over.

I stepped in front of her. "You've got to understand. I really believe he's different."

Liz shrugged her shoulders. "So?"

"Liz, you are my friend, aren't you? Please promise not to tell."

"Am I your friend?" She stomped her foot down hard on the floor. "Seems like if you were my friend you wouldn't have gone off without a word on the most important day of my life."

"Liz, we're talking about a person's life here, a special, talented person." Even before Liz reached around me for the doorknob and I saw her face, I knew I was doing a miserable job of playing set-the-table. "I'm sorry about the recital, Liz. I really am. I hate how I hurt you."

But Liz interrupted. "You're not sorry. You're just worried about your precious Ethan. Get out of my room, Clare Armstrong." She pointed toward the door. "Get out of my house. You and your crazy boyfriend make me sick. Just get out of here."

"Liz," I begged. "Please." She turned her head away.

Outside on the road I stood looking at my arms and hands. They weren't moving, but on the inside I felt a sort of all-over shaking just like I had after the accident. I glanced at the house. Maybe I should go back in there and threaten Liz, or maybe I should cry more and try again to apologize.

I wanted to sit down by the side of the road to think. Time. That would be best. Liz couldn't stay mad very long.

I turned toward Ethan's house but changed my mind. The Ford was in the driveway, meaning his parents were home, but what prevented me from crossing the grass to knock on his door was dread of seeing Ethan as he had been when he crawled from our car and moved in a sleepwalk toward home.

Tomorrow. Tomorrow, I would check on Ethan. I walked toward home, but stopped, hearing him call my name. Even from the sound of his voice, I knew he was back.

Whirling, I watched him run to me. Inside was a huge piece of lead where my heart had been. Oh, our precious day! How long ago it seemed. It was gone, leaving me with a terrible knowledge. Ethan was back, but I had watched as he had stepped away from me into the dark, and now because of me everyone might find out.

I reached out to touch the bandage on his forehead. "You're okay, aren't you?"

"Sure." He put his arms around me, and I leaned against him for a minute. Then thinking that Dad might somehow see us, I moved away.

"Dad didn't kill me." I tried to speak lightly. "How about you?"

He rubbed the back of his neck. "They were pretty worked up at first, but they sort of cooled down. Dad said they should have let me start driving again as soon as the medicine got cut. They've even said I can drive to school sometimes when the Rambler is fixed."

I had not expected his parents, having watched his suffering, to be hard on him. I wanted to say something right out, but it had to be quick because suppertime was near. "I'm glad you'll get the car, but I can't ride with you again until I'm sixteen, which is next spring. I promised God."

"God?" Ethan raised his eyebrows.

It would be necessary, I knew, to explain about the journal and the promise, but I wasn't ready. Suddenly I felt extremely tired. My impulse was to claim to have meant Dad rather than God, but I stopped myself. Not lying, ever, would not be easy.

"I made a promise to God," I said. "I'll tell you about it tomorrow, but right now I can't be late for supper."

After I ate, I put the peacock feather on the wall of my room with tacks. I would try to remember the good parts of the day, but I would also remember my truth pledge. Then, exhausted, I fell asleep.

On Sunday afternoon as soon as I finished the dinner dishes, I headed for the swings. Ethan waited on a bench. I saw him there drawing in the dirt with a stick, and I stood still for a moment watching until he looked up and smiled.

"Ethan." My voice shook when I said his name. "Liz knows all about your illness. She read it in my journal. I shouldn't have written any of it down. It was a stupid thing to do." Choking back a sob, I went over to flop into a swing.

He too took a swing and reached for my hand. He said nothing at first, just stared at the lines he had made in the dirt with the stick. I saw that he made music notes. Then he shrugged his shoulders. "Don't worry about it. Of course you had to write it down. You're a writer, remember?"

"I'm so sorry." It was becoming quite a familiar comment. "I really don't think Liz will tell."

"Well, it isn't such a big deal really. It was my folks' idea, moving here and not telling anyone. I went along with it because it seemed easier. People will all know anyway if I go back to the hospital."

I gripped the swing chain and tried not to let the fear show in my voice. "What do you mean? Is something wrong?"

"He's back. I heard Friedrich's voice last night when I sat down at the piano. I'm getting sick again, I guess. I haven't told my parents." His voice broke. "They'll be so upset."

I jumped from the swing. "No. I can't believe it. You're fine now. All the time we waited at the police station I thought about what my dad would say. Maybe that's the way it was with you, just thinking about Friedrich. Couldn't that be it?"

Ethan lowered his head. "No, I'm afraid not. I didn't imagine Friedrich. He seemed very real to me. He was angry, said things about how I should have been practicing instead of chasing around with a foolish girl."

"Me foolish?" I tried to make Ethan smile, but it didn't work.

Ethan kept his head down. "Friedrich said my dad would probably take the piano away completely. He's been so hateful since I started trying to block him out."

An idea started forming in my mind. I walked away from the swings and went to sit on the bench. "Don't tell anyone about Friedrich, not yet. Maybe it was just the stress from the accident and all." I chewed at my lip, thinking hard.

"I don't know." He stood up and began to pace.

"Ethan," I said, "what does Friedrich want from you?"

"For me to write his concerto down. He wants me to get it on paper so it will be saved for the world."

"What if you quit trying to block him out? Maybe if you wrote down the notes it would all be over."

He came to sit beside me. "You're talking like he's real instead of some quirk in my mind."

I shrugged. "We don't know for sure what he is, but maybe it doesn't make any difference. Maybe if you write down the music, he will go away."

"I don't want to go back to that hospital. I really, really don't." He drew his knees up to his chest and grasped them hard.

I wanted to scream, but I kept my voice steady. Not even caring if someone saw me, I put my arms around him. "It's worth a try," I said. "We've got to try something."

TWELVE

I should have known as soon as we got off the bus on Monday that the news of Ethan's illness was out. A group of kids around the front door got quiet when we approached. "Bet they're discussing our fatal trip to the city," I told him.

In English Mr. Elliot gave an assignment I really liked. We were supposed to copy favorite poems, write paragraphs discussing them, and find or draw illustrations. I sat considering what poems to use when Rosemary Williams pushed a note at me from behind.

Asking for help already, I thought, but I was wrong. The words jumped up at me. "They say that Ethan is nuts, just out of a mental hospital. True? R.W."

I wadded the note in my shaking hand. For just a

second I felt like I might faint. Mr. Elliot, at the front of the room, began to fade in and out of sight.

Anger saved me. Across the aisle sat Liz, pushing the cuticles on one hand back with the thumbnail of the other. Never had I experienced true hatred, but I felt it burst like a flame igniting inside me.

Grabbing a piece of paper from my notebook, I printed, "I hate you, Liz. I always will."

"Liz," I whispered, not worried about who heard me. When she glanced my way, I held up the message. Tears filled her eyes, but they did nothing to douse the fire within me.

"You may have the rest of the period to work on the assignment, using the books on the back shelves," said Mr. Elliot. He started to move around the room.

I made no effort to get a book. "Not working?" Mr. Elliot asked when he passed my desk. I shook my head. He knew about my love for poetry and wouldn't feel the need to push me.

"I don't feel very well," I told him. It sure was the truth, not that it mattered any more about lying. God obviously had no interest in making deals with me.

"Wait," Liz called when the bell rang, but I shot up and toward the door. I did not turn back.

The hall seemed fuller than usual, bodies every-where blocking my way to the science room. I was near the door when Ethan, lips pressed into a tight smile, came out.

We looked at each other. "You've heard, huh," he said. "Don't worry. I'm not going to let this get me down." His face was pale.

All around us kids slammed lockers, louder than I had ever noticed. "Sure," I almost screamed. "I know you won't." I wanted to take his hand, but my arms were full of books.

Except for the white face, Ethan did seem all right, better able to handle the problem than I was. Still, I worried. My stomach hurting violently, I slumped in my world history seat and only shook my head dumbly in response to the teacher's question about Charlemagne.

In the cafeteria at lunch, I heard some snickering from the kids at one table as we walked by to get in line. I whirled around to look at them. They stopped laughing and just looked down. Ethan took my arm and led me through the line.

No one sat at the table with us until Motie Ann dropped beside me. She didn't realize anything was wrong and started telling us right off about going with her little niece and nephew to a carnival in Edmond. "The merry-go-round had swans," she said, and she smiled. It made me feel good to see that smile, and I think it helped Ethan too.

We were stacking our trays with the others when Ethan suggested the piano. "Let's go to the auditorium," he said. "I'd like to play a little."

Mrs. Pulley, on hall duty, did not object, so Motie Ann and I took seats in the front row. Ethan began at once. I got out my library book and did not notice when Motie Ann slipped from her seat and went to stand behind Ethan.

"Do you like music?" he asked, and she nodded her head. When I glanced up next, Motie Ann sat on the bench beside Ethan, who explained to her about octaves and notes.

Before the bell rang, Motie Ann was putting out hesitant fingers to touch the keys. "Can we do this some more times?" she asked, and Ethan assured her we would do it often. It was okay with me. Better to spend the lunch break with a good book and music. We three didn't really belong outside with those laughing others.

I dreaded the period after lunch, girls' athletics. I was bound to come face to face with Liz. The group sat in a semicircle, the coach the focal point of all eyes. He talked for a while about how the gym floor had to have a new finish before the first game. "It's not far away," he said. "I'm passing out suits today."

Because the school had no football team, all of Collins Creek waited for our first basketball game. A few days earlier, being a starter in that game had been really important to me. As the coach spoke, playing on the main string, even playing at all, meant nothing. Not until I glanced at Liz, who looked intently at the coach's face.

"We'll both try real hard," I remembered Liz had said about the starting position on the main team.

"Now the thing to keep in mind," Coach Alexander said, "is this. What matters is not who starts or who plays the most. We've got to be a team. We work together."

He was wrong. What mattered to me was only one thing. It mattered that I beat Liz for the important open spot. I fastened my eyes on her and waited for her to feel my stare. With my hand in front of my breastbone I moved my thumb just enough to point toward myself. I would beat Liz out of that place one way or another, and my look expressed, I hoped, total contempt.

The tears were in Liz's eyes again. "You can have the starting place," she mouthed to me. Then her hand went up. "Coach—" Her voice sounded unfamiliar. "I don't want to play this year. Can I keep the scoreboard?"

Rage exploded inside me like a dry log being added to a blazing campfire. I sat with clenched fists while the suits were passed out, and I followed slowly when the others rushed to the locker room to try them on.

It was a long afternoon, and I couldn't even take joy in the final dismissal because of the bus ride ahead.

"Let's walk," I suggested to Ethan, who waited for me at my locker.

"No." He shook his head. "We can't walk all year. May as well get it over with." We moved into the stream of kids getting on buses.

The driver, Mr. Griffith, supplemented his store income by delivery of scholars to and from school. Fortunately the Collins Creek district contained no railroad tracks. Mr. Griffith, perhaps because of his years on a bus full of kids, would never have heard a train. Nor did he hear Melvin Erikson.

"Hey, Looney Tunes," Melvin yelled as we pushed our way down the aisle. "Weave any baskets lately?" There was a great burst of laughter, which Melvin punctuated with a catcall.

I stepped on some little kid's feet, but we shoved

our way into a seat near the front. When the bus motor started, Ethan began to hum softly to himself. I took his hand, but he barely glanced at me.

I tried to concentrate on the death of Old Sunny. It was, compared to the day we had just endured, an easier memory.

When we got off the bus, I noticed Liz wasn't there. Hope she's been kidnapped, I thought. Ethan and I stood talking for a few minutes on the road in front of his house. I made a little pit in the gravel with the toe of my brown loafer. "It's my fault," I said. "I'd give anything if I could fix it."

Ethan brushed my hair from my eyes. "No big deal," he said. "They'll find someone else to laugh at after a while."

I looked up to study his face. "If Friedrich tries to come tonight, will you let him?"

"I'm ready for him," he said, and he laughed. "Maybe I'll invite him to come to school with us."

At home I went to my room without going to the kitchen or calling hello. Even before I threw my books on the bed, I heard a knock.

"May I come in, Clare?" Mom spoke softly, and I had no doubt that she had heard the story. Our community, having no newspaper, television, or radio station, still spread information as quick as lightning.

If they say I can't see him, I told myself, I'll just say right out that I will anyway. They can't stop me without really locking me in this room.

"Clare?"

"Come in." I answered my mother's softness with determination, and I turned sharply to face her. "Mom, I won't stop being his friend. I'm not going to, no matter what Dad says either."

Mom pulled me to her and began to stroke my hair. "Don't cry," she said, tears filling her own eyes. "No one in this family is living in the Dark Ages. We'll not turn that boy from our door." In her voice was a certain quality. It was not often there, but I had heard it on a few occasions. I knew that even if my father did not agree, it would make no difference.

When I went into the kitchen later, Mom fretted about her shortage of hamburger. "I hate to ask you to ride down there, but they usually have fresh meat at Griffith's on Monday."

My bike had a flat tire, but needing to move, to work out the nervous cramps in my body, I didn't mind walking. Teddy wanted to go too.

It was not an unpleasant walk, the September sun having lost some of its ability to assault by late afternoon. "Look at the puppies," Teddy said, pointing at the little balls of fur that bounced off the porch of the McGuires' farmhouse. "You think they are going to give them away?"

"They're probably too little to leave their mother," I said and changed the subject. "You want me to play basketball with you when we get home?"

Inside the store five men sat at the counter, but I didn't catch the usual political discussion. I ordered the hamburger meat, and Mrs. Griffith started to wrap it in white paper and tie it with the twine suspended from the ceiling on a spool. That's when I realized what the topic of discussion really was.

Only a genuine nut in the community could have brought two roustabouts, a pumper, a gauger, and even a straw boss into such an open, equal conversation.

"Real strange," one of them said. "A kid being like that. It's real strange."

"Dangerous, too. A kid nuts that way. He's not safe for the others to be around." It was the pumper Jess Russell. Jess Russell, who no girl at church would walk by for fear he would reach out and hug her too tight, sat there calling Ethan dangerous.

I jumped from my stool. "You filthy old man," I screamed. "You filthy, filthy old man." Turning, I ran out the door and over the pop bottle caps toward home.

After a time I slowed to wait for Teddy, who, having stayed for the meat, was trying to catch up with me. On his face was a look of pity mixed with fear.

"What's wrong, Clare? Why'd you do that?" He thrust the white bundle into my hand, which still held the money. Griffith's would wait until next time for payment.

"I'm all right, Teddy. But you just don't pay any attention to a lot of stupid talk." My eyes fell to the package. Penciled in black on the white paper was a message from Mrs. Griffith: "Some of the craziest people in the world are them that set around calling other folks nuts."

It was the note that gave me strength for school the next day. Not everyone in Collins Creek was narrow-minded and ignorant, I told myself; and things weren't so bad after a while. Ethan and I stayed pretty much to ourselves except for Motie Ann. Every day at lunch we went into the auditorium for music, and amazingly Motie Ann began to pick up techniques quickly.

"She's got some real talent," Ethan told me. "She'd have to, to learn so fast."

Those were gentle times. Music filled the auditorium, and I read my book. One day I turned around and realized there were other kids there listening, maybe as many as fifteen of them scattered around in different places.

Like Ethan had predicted, talk died down fairly soon. It wasn't long until the girls, unable to be distrustful of such good looks, began to hang around Ethan again.

"I mean," I heard Sheila Olsen say in the gym one afternoon, "I was knocked cold when Liz called to tell me. I wouldn't go out with him or anything, but what harm can there be in talking?"

I stepped from the shower with only a towel around me. "You're darn right," I yelled. "You sure wouldn't go out with him or anything, because he wouldn't be caught dead with you."

"Sometimes," said Sheila disdainfully, "I think you are the crazy one, not Ethan."

On a Sunday in early October, Ethan and I took a picnic lunch to the trees at the back of Johnson's pasture.

Walking through the grass, we startled a group of

quail. We watched the little brown birds scatter. "My dad hunts them during season," I said. "They sure are good."

"My dad does too," said Ethan. "I like to eat them, but I just can't get interested in hunting."

"Talk about hunting—" I pointed above our heads to a group of flying ducks. Faint cries reached our ears from their U formation. "Wouldn't some hunter like a crack at them."

He stopped walking and stared at the ducks. "I hope they make it south without getting shot."

I watched them too, tracing their line with my finger. "Ducks going south. A sure sign that fall is coming."

Ethan took my hand. "It's almost over. Summer is gone." His voice sounded sad.

"But we have fall and winter and spring, then summer again," I said. He smiled at me, but said nothing.

When we spread the picnic cloth on a level spot, I began to take tuna sandwiches out of our basket. "Clare," he said, "I want to tell you about Friedrich."

I did not put the sandwich down. Instead, I held it tight. "You've heard him again?"

Ethan nodded his head slowly. "Last night. I told him I'd write down the music. I asked him if he would leave me alone then, and he said maybe he would." He paused for a minute and looked up at the sky before he went on. "Friedrich is worried that something will happen to me before the music is finished."

Ethan stood up and walked around the picnic cloth. "He isn't there, not really." He dropped to his knees beside me. "Clare, maybe I'd better tell my folks."

I reached out and took his arm. "Ethan, we can't be certain he's not real. Of course your folks say he isn't. Mine would say the same thing. Mr. Elliot would too. But how do we know for sure? Write the music down, Ethan. Give it a try."

I leaned my face against his arm. I wanted to stay that way, me fastened to Ethan. I wanted to hold on, to keep him from slipping away.

THIRTEEN

At school on Monday, we decided to have lunch at Griffith's. The store was crowded, but Ethan and I found two empty stools at the end of the counter. When Liz came in, I studied her. She was walking with Barbara Fisher. They laughed about something, and for just a second I cared what.

When she came toward me, I stared straight at her, daring her to speak. She stopped right beside my stool. "Clare," she said softly. "Please."

I turned away and began to tap the fingers of one hand rapidly on the counter while I used the other to shove my hamburger into my mouth. From the corner of my eye I saw Ethan move. Leaning behind me, he held out his hand to Liz.

She took his hand. "I'm sorry I told," she said.

"It's okay," he answered.

A bomb of anger discharged inside, throwing me to my feet. With one quick swoop, I pushed aside Ethan's arm. Ignoring Liz, I turned violently on him. "You've just got to be the great forgiver, don't you? Who do you think you are, some saint or something?"

I didn't intend to drop my hamburger, but neither did I make any attempt to pick it up. With my eyes fastened on the door, not looking at anyone and closing my ears to their voices, somehow I made my way outside and across the street to the school ground.

Only the dropped hamburger bothered me. Since her note, I had considered Mrs. Griffith a special ally, and I hated having just spread my lunch all over her floor. Ethan, I thought, was probably cleaning it up before he came looking for me. He didn't come.

Motie Ann found me in the hall. "Where's Ethan?" she asked. "It's time for the piano."

I wanted to scream at her to leave me alone, but I didn't. "Let's go on in," I said. "He'll be along soon, I think."

Motie Ann went right to the piano, and I took a seat

near the front as usual. She messed with the keys, and I listened, surprised that I could recognize pieces of tunes that she played. Ethan did not come.

"The music's not good without Ethan," Motie Ann said when the bell rang, and I stomped away from her.

I walked on to the gym alone and was the first one to be dressed for scrimmage. When Liz came in, she went without a glance at me, up into the bleachers where the scoreboard keeper sat at a special table.

Between each of my afternoon classes, I expected Ethan to come to find me, but he didn't. I was cooling down. Before algebra, I decided I would apologize when I got the chance. After all, it was natural that he wouldn't be as mad at Liz as I was. I was the one who had been betrayed by her.

When school was out, I thought I'd wait for Ethan at the bus, but when I got there, I saw that he was already there and getting on with Liz. I stopped and stared as they boarded, talking. The ride home was miserable, but when we stopped at the camp gate, I made sure I got off and was well on my way home before they had time to unload.

Furious, I kicked at the gravel as I marched home.

Teddy, having passed me on the way, was already at the kitchen table when I came in. "Chocolate chip cookies," he said, pouring two glasses of milk.

"No thanks." I headed to my room with Mom behind me.

"They're still hot," she said.

I shook my head.

"Is something wrong, dear?"

I shook my head again. Then tossing my books on my bed, I followed her out of my room. "I'm going outside for a while," I said. How could I tell anyone that Ethan, after all we had been through, was dropping me for another girl?

A couple of preschoolers were in the sandbox, but I didn't say anything to them. For a while I sat in the swing trying to get my mind on the weather. It was not so hot. Fall was definitely about to arrive.

When King came running toward me, I wanted to kick at him and yell get, but I couldn't. Wagging his tail, he looked at me with loyal devotion. It was a quality obviously missing in his master, whom I ignored until I had petted the dog.

"Where's your friend Liz?" I kept my eyes on the dog. "Did you run your finger up her nose?" Ethan and

I had laughed about the nose story, but I wasn't laughing as I looked up at him this time.

Silently, he returned my gaze. I gave myself a push, but he reached out to stop me by grabbing the chain. With his other hand he pulled me from the swing and to my feet.

"Hey, what's——" I was interrupted by his lips over mine as he pulled me to him, where I rested for a minute in total shock.

Embarrassed, thrilled, I stepped back. "That was a surprise," I said, and I shook my head.

"Why?" He gave me a big grin. "Who do you think I am, some kind of saint?"

There was a spark in his eye, and I became suspicious that the whole thing, staying away from me, riding the bus with Liz, was designed to get to me. "You wanted to make me jealous to get even for what I did at Griffith's?" I accused when we had settled back in the swings.

"Maybe the thought crossed my mind." He grinned. "But I don't see any reason to be mad at Liz. Clare, I don't want you to throw away a friendship on account of me."

I studied at the dirt beneath my swing. Maybe I could let go of the anger. Maybe it had just about burned itself out. "I'll think about it," I said. Liz obviously wanted to be friends again, and most of the talk about Ethan's illness seemed to have died down.

For a while we didn't talk. I gave myself a push and started swinging fairly high. Ethan kept his swing still, and he sort of stared off in front of him.

"If Friedrich comes tonight, we can finish the music," he said.

I quit pumping my legs and let the swing slow down. "Do you think he will?" I asked.

Ethan nodded. "I can feel him, sort of waiting at the edge of my mind."

"When you finish, you may be free of him." Inside I had already started to pray. "Please, God. Please, God, no more hospitals."

A strange little laugh came from Ethan. "I guess you can't think I'm any crazier than you already do, so I can tell you. I'll sort of miss him if he goes away."

"It's okay," I said. "You miss him all you want, but you let him go." Quit trying to play psychiatrist, I thought, but I didn't stop. "You tell him good-bye to-night."

Of course I couldn't get my mind on homework. Sitting on the porch after supper, I tried to write in my journal to sort out what Ethan had said about Friedrich, but I couldn't get down how it really was, the sadness in Ethan's voice when he talked about Friedrich's going, or the awful icy fear that coated my insides.

I stayed out until it was too dark to write. The pump still beat in competition with night sounds, but now there was a definite coolness in the air. After an Oklahoma scorcher, most people long for fall, but suddenly the loss of summer seemed terribly sad. I walked over the playground and picked the biggest sunflower I could find to take into my room and put it in a fruit-jar vase.

FOURTEEN

There was nothing about the next day to hint that it would live always in the memory of all Collins Creek. Waking early, I lay in bed entertaining myself with the lash that had come away on my hand as I rubbed my eye. It was an old, almost forgotten game, but I revived it that morning with a passion. With the lash pressed between my thumb and index finger, I would close my eyes and pose a question. If the lash stuck to the thumb, the answer was yes, to the index finger was a no.

My questions all centered around Ethan. Would he kiss me again soon? Was Friedrich only in his mind? The most important question of all: Would he have to go back to the hospital? When an answer was not to my liking, I declared it a best-three-out-of-five solution.

Finally my mother called for me to get up, and I rose with a misguided feeling that what lay ahead would be an especially good day. In honor of the promise of fall in the air, I chose a dress of dark plaid. Spending more time than usual on my hair, I didn't get to the bus stop until the bus was in sight.

Ethan waited for me to get on with him. "Clare plus Ethan," Teddy chanted from in front of us.

I threw a tissue at him. "If you say that in front of Dad, I'll break your neck." I knew he wouldn't. Even at nine Teddy understood a lot of things.

When we had found a seat, I studied Ethan's face for hints of strain. I wanted to ask about Friedrich, but the crowded bus wasn't a place for a discussion. Still, I didn't have to wonder about it long.

"Look," he said. He took a sheet filled with musical notes from his notebook. At the top was written "Forest Concerto."

I gasped, and he squeezed my hand. "I'll play it at noon," he said.

"Good," I said. My stomach was in knots, and I wanted to calm down. I turned my head to stare out the window. The McGuires' yard gave me something to think about. "Wonder how much longer those roses will stay on that bush." I pointed at the big bush of red flowers beside the front porch.

"Oh, I bet they last a while," he said. "They look like they've got a lot of life in them yet."

"So do those puppies," I said, and then we both saw the sign. "Free pups."

"Hey," said Ethan. "I know what I'll do. I'm going to get you a present."

I shook my head. "How about a stuffed dog instead? One to set on my bed."

"Just like a woman," he teased. "Stuffed dogs cost money. The sign says these are free. Think about it, okay? I'll even let you pick it out."

"Gosh," I said, "your generosity overwhelms me."

At school I thought of nothing but Ethan's music and his encounters with Friedrich. My stomach bothered me so much during second-period class that I was afraid I might throw up. Mr. Elliot excused me from class. I leaned on the sink and waited until the sickness passed.

Mr. Elliot frowned on long absences from class. I was about to go back to class when I looked up at the mirror and noticed brown oxfords showing beneath the door of the last stall. Only one girl in school wore shoes like those oxfords, and she was sitting on the floor in that stall. "Motie Ann," I said. "What are you doing in there?"

"Just staying," was the tearful reply.

"Why? Why are you just staying on the floor?"

"I ain't going to go back to class today, not none."

I stepped up on the stool in the next stall and was able to look down at her. "Why? Tell me what's wrong."

The face she turned up to me was pitiful. "Them boys. Started on me again. Saying would I come behind the bus barn with them at noon. Saying they would vote for me for homecoming queen if I would meet them behind the barn and let them touch me." She pointed to her lumpy breasts. "They want to touch me where they shouldn't. I ain't going back to class."

"Motie Ann, come on out. I'll help you." I jumped down and pulled at the door, wondering how I would keep my promise.

"No. I'm not going to come out till it's time to go home."

"You can't do that," I said. I fanned the air around me with my hand. "Gosh, that stuff they're putting on the gym floor stinks. Gives me a headache."

Our girls' rest room connected to the gym, and it was also used as the girls' locker room. A new lacquer had just been applied to make the floor ready for the first basketball game.

"Come on, Motie, or some teacher will come and get you. You can't just stay here."

"They ain't going to make me open this door. I ain't going to do it neither."

Maybe I should go back and tell Mr. Elliot what was going on, but just then we heard the door open.

I sure didn't want anyone else involved. "Pull in your feet, Motie Ann," I whispered.

Karen Preston came in. I busied myself with washing my hands. Then, just in case, I stood in front of Motie Ann's stall to dry them on the paper towel.

Karen pulled a cigarette from her purse. "I didn't know you smoked," I said. I looked in the mirror; no sign of brown oxfords. Motie Ann had them up.

"Shush," Karen leaned her head toward the door leading to the gym. "Coach might be in there."

"Well," I said quietly. "I am surprised to see you with a cigarette since you're on the main string, that's all."

"Yeah?" Karen took a deep pull on her Winston. "Lots of people are surprised to see you hanging around with a crazy boy and a retard."

A roll of toilet paper sailed over the stall. In the mirror I saw the top of Motie Ann's red hair disappear. She was a good shot; the paper hit Karen in the head.

"Hey, what's the big idea?"

"Don't you go calling me that," Motie said from inside the stall.

"You stupid idiot." Karen rubbed her head. "I'll get even with you for this." She kicked at the toilet paper on the floor.

I had to think quick. "Calm down, Karen," I said gently. "You aren't hurt. Motie Ann wouldn't want to hurt you."

A grunt of disagreement came from behind the stall.

"Well," Karen made a swipe at the sink with her cigarette before dropping it in the tall trash container near the gym door. "That retard needs to be taught a lesson."

If only I had paid more attention to Karen's cigarette. If only I'd noticed that she hadn't put it out carefully. But I didn't.

I reached for Karen's arm. "If you cause any trouble over this, I'll go straight to the coach about you smoking."

Her eyes spit anger at me. "Boy, Clare, you've sure changed since you got involved with the crazies." She jerked her arm away and walked out. I was glad because I had very nearly slapped her.

I was more than a little exasperated with Motie Ann. "I've got to go back to class," I told her. She was sitting on the floor again. "Here"—I kicked the roll of paper toward her—"you might need this. If you don't come out pretty soon, some teacher will be in here after you." There was a noise just outside. "Here comes someone now." I moved toward the door.

"I'll come out at noon," Motie Ann called. "I'll come for the music. You tell Ethan and that other boy too, the one in the funny clothes."

I whirled back. "What?" and then I saw Mrs. Pulley, the home economics teacher.

"Were you saying something, Clare?" She stomped into the rest room, her nose wrinkled. "I want to check those fumes. They're too strong, even fill the hall. I think they've overdone it with that lacquer. It's not safe." She stood there, her arms crossed, and I got the feeling she wasn't going to be leaving soon.

"No, I just coughed," I said, and I coughed again. "Got to get back to class."

"Clare," Mr. Elliot said when I slipped back into my

seat. "We're just having a little quiz. Question number one is, Define metaphor."

I caught up and was ready for number two. Mr. Elliot opened his mouth, but we never heard the question because the room rocked with a big blast. There were sounds of screams and the smell of smoke.

Mr. Elliot's face turned white, but his voice was steady. "You must stay calm." He stepped to the door and looked into the hall. "Fire drill procedure. Straight line. No pushing. No running. There must have been an accident."

From behind me I heard sobs. "Stay calm," Mr. Elliot said again. "Pull yourself together and be brave." There was something in his voice. The crying stopped.

Out in the hall, I saw Ethan coming with his science class. He stepped out of that line and got in front of me. "Hold on to my belt," he said, "so we stay together."

Worried about Teddy, I strained to look toward the elementary section. The smoke wasn't so thick down that way, and I figured he would be okay.

The line slowed for a minute in front of the rest room, and I remembered Motie Ann. I jerked Ethan's belt. "I think Motie Ann's in there," I said, and I pointed.

We left the line, and Ethan pushed open the door. A crying sound came from the stall.

The back wall of the rest room was gone, and we could see the gym engulfed in flames. The smoke was so thick, we could hardly see Motie Ann crouched on the floor where I had left her.

I opened my mouth to tell her to get up, but Ethan had already yanked her to her feet. We had to hold our breath and feel our way to the door.

Out in the hall the smoke wasn't quite so bad. We could breathe a little better. I couldn't see anyone and figured the lines must have speeded up. "Get down and crawl," Ethan said, and we did.

We could see the light from the outside door when Ethan suddenly stopped and turned around. "You two go on," he told me. "I'm going back to my locker. I've got to get the music."

"No," I said, and I reached out to grab at him, but he was up and running. "No," I screamed, "you said, 'Hold on.' You said we'd stay together."

The smoke was pretty thick by then, and I felt Motie Ann move more than I saw her. "I'll go with you, Ethan," she yelled. "I'll go with you for the music."

"No," I screamed. "No, come back." I coughed and

wiped at my eyes. Follow them, I thought, but I couldn't see anything except smoke. Before I could get myself to move, they were both gone. I turned and started to crawl in their direction.

But my head pounded, and all the energy went out of me. Maybe I should go for help instead. My breath came hard, and I just let myself go into a heap on the floor. Probably I would have stayed right there except for Mr. Elliot.

Even though they were just in front of my face, I barely saw the legs of his pants because they were the same gray pants he wore almost every day to school. They nearly blended into the smoke.

"Clare," he screamed.

I reached out and touched at his leg. "Help me find Ethan and Motie Ann," I gasped.

"We've got to get you out first." He dropped beside me and pulled. At first I held back, but he only jerked harder. He didn't talk, just crawled toward the door. Every once in a while he would reach out and drag me up beside him. I wanted to resist, but no strength came to me.

The crowd was a long way from the building, but I heard them cheer when we came out the door. I also heard a fire siren.

Some teachers ran toward us. "Ethan," I screamed. "You've got to help Ethan and Motie Ann."

"There's a lot of smoke in there," said Coach Alexander, and he shook his head with doubt. Just then the fire truck pulled up. Someone led me away, but I kept looking back at the firemen with their ladders and equipment.

My head felt real funny, like I might faint, but I kept looking at the faces of the kids, wanting to be sure that Liz was okay. I spotted her just as Teddy came running to me. He was crying. I grabbed him and held on tight. "They're getting Ethan right now," I said, "and Motie Ann. They'll be all right. The firemen know how to help them." I felt very cold, like the middle of winter.

Parents started coming for their children. Some men from the sheriff's office kept people back, but when the firemen brought out two stretchers, I pushed around a guard and ran toward them. I could see Motie Ann's brown oxford sticking from beneath one sheet. It was the only thing visible. The heads on both stretchers were covered.

I didn't scream or cry or anything. Feeling even colder, I just stood there, hugging my sobbing little brother until our parents came.

Isn't it strange to see Dad cry? I thought on the way

to the car. He kept his arms around Teddy and me as we walked. It helped me feel a little warmer.

"It was smoke," I heard Mom say to Dad. "I'm glad they didn't burn."

"Could have been so much worse. Could have lost more than two real easy," Dad said.

I looked down at the plaid in my dress. The white part had turned gray.

At home everything seemed odd. My own room had an unfamiliar look to it. Mom said I'd feel better if I cried. Willing to do anything to improve my state, I would gladly have let go had there been any tears to release, not that I believed crying would help.

I knew what my mother did not. There would be no escape from the strange coldness. Even in bed with a blanket I still shivered.

"You have company." Mom stood in my door, and Liz half hid behind her. "Go on in, dear." Mom put her arm around Liz and sort of guided her into the room.

Liz moved slowly over to stand by my bed. "I guess you must hate me more than ever now," she said.

I looked right into her eyes that were red from crying. "I don't hate you anymore." It came out in a whisper. "I don't feel anything but cold."

"I was so scared when you didn't come out. I wanted to go back for you, but Mr. Elliot wouldn't let me. And I'm sorry about Ethan. Oh, Clare, I'm so awful sorry."

I nodded my head. She dropped down to the floor beside my bed, and I saw her moving the rosary that she held in her hand. I guess I must have gone to sleep then, because the next thing I knew Liz was gone, and Dr. Cleveland was there with his stethoscope wanting me to breathe for him.

I couldn't believe he had come all the way from Edmond. My wound wasn't one he could bandage. "She'll be fine tomorrow," he said to my folks.

I wanted to scream that I would never be fine again, but I couldn't pull up the strength. I just turned my face away from them to look at the wall.

The doctor prescribed some relaxation medication. After he left, I ate some soup, took the pill, and spent the night swimming through strange, cold dreams.

Mom woke me with a breakfast tray. Sitting in my wicker chair, she talked about the arrangements. Ethan's funeral would be at our church the next morning. For Motie Ann there would be no local service. Her burial would be in the eastern part of the state, near the graves of her father and grandparents.

Mom reached over to spread jam on my toast. "Would you want to see Motie Ann? Pay our respects at the funeral home before they move her?"

I picked up the toast and looked at it. "I guess. I guess I should." I could eat nothing from the tray.

"Oh," said Mom when we were on the road. "I'll have to stop for gas." I could tell from her voice that she was reluctant to stop at Griffith's, causing me to stare across at the school.

From the outside no damage was visible. Even the gym had lost only its interior, but because of weak walls and smoke damage there would be no school for a time. It was all because of the fumes and Karen's cigarette. She had even told the story herself—but none of that mattered to me.

Looking at the building did not cause me pain. If they would let me, I would like to go back inside to find the place where they died. I would sit there for a long time and try to find something to fill the cold emptiness inside.

At the funeral home we signed a guest book. A few

teachers' names were written there. Probably there would not be many visitors. I wished all those who had taunted her could be forced to look on her body, lifeless but pretty.

"Don't her hair look nice?" Mrs. Rawlings asked me. "A regular beauty parlor woman done it."

Her hair did look good, red curls arranged softly around a face that had been, before death, too highly colored. Redheads don't wear pink, I had always thought, but the person who chose Motie Ann's pink nightgown obviously knew better.

"She looks pretty," I told her mother. They were the only words of comfort I could offer.

"Ethan's here too," my mother said, but she did not press against my refusal.

I doubted that I would ever be able to look at a dead Ethan. The coldness inside me was beginning to slip a little, being replaced by a misery deep enough to make me hope it would be fatal.

"I may not go to his funeral," I told my mother. We had just gotten into the car.

"I think that would be a mistake. You need to face your grief."

"I may not go," I said again, longing for the coldness to return. "I should have stayed," I moaned, and I leaned against the window.

Mom opened her door. "We can go back in."

"No," I groaned. "Not in there! I should have stayed in the school with Ethan."

"Oh, no, darling." My mother pulled me into her arms. "Oh, no, don't ever think that. No, oh, no."

All the way home, I felt the agony growing inside me. Saying nothing, I huddled on my side of the car, arms wrapped around my own body with my eyes closed. I put my head back on the seat, blotting out everything until we stopped in front of the Benningtons' house.

"It might comfort them to see you." Mom reached for my hand, but I pulled away.

"No," I held to the car door handle on my side. "No, I can't."

"Please, Clare. It might help you and them." She brushed at my hair with her hand.

There were several cars in the driveway and some strangers in the living room. I did not look at any of them, only at Mrs. Bennington, who came weeping to take me in her arms. I stood very still, afraid that if I started to cry, I would never, never stop.

Finally, she stepped away from me. "Just a minute, Clare. I have something for you."

She returned, took my hand, and closed my fingers over an object, cool and round. Ethan's ring lay in my palm.

"He would want you to have it."

I tightened my fingers over the ring. "He was so special," I said. "Just so awful special." I edged toward the door. "Thank you for the ring," I murmured before I slipped out.

Not waiting for Mom and a ride in the car, I ran as fast as I could through the camp, through the playground, and out into Johnson's pasture, where I threw myself on the brown grass under a cottonwood tree. I slid the ring on my finger, moving it to catch the sun in the red stone. For a short time I listened to the caw of a crow and the beat of the oil pump. Then all other sounds were lost to me, covered by the wildness of my sorrow.

Later, Teddy came for me. "Let's go home," he said, leading me by the hand like he was my big brother.

Inside the house, I took down the kitchen calendar. "I want to count the days," I told my mother, and I took it with me to my room.

I put my pencil on July 12, 1960, the day Ethan

moved into our camp, and I counted. "Ninety days," I said. "I only knew him ninety days." It didn't seem possible. I left the calendar on my desk and went over to stare at myself in the dresser mirror. My face was different because of Ethan. My eyes saw things they would never have noticed before. Down inside me, my heart beat stronger and sent stronger blood out to my fingers and toes.

I studied my fifteen-year-old self. Ethan, I thought, will never get older. I will probably be an old lady someday with wrinkled skin and gray hair. So will Liz. Even then, when I am some kid's grandma, I will remember Ethan. Sometimes on summer nights I will want to talk about him, and of course I will talk to Liz, because she will remember him too.

Standing there in front of my dresser, I made some decisions. I would ask the Benningtons if I could go through Ethan's notebook, and I would take the *Forest Concerto*. Maybe Friedrich was only in Ethan's mind. Maybe he was a real boy who had slipped through the curtain of time. I wasn't likely to ever know now, but someday I would do something with that music. Someday I would make sure the world had a chance to hear it.

Ethan had told me once that a concerto was a piece

written to feature one instrument. That's what his life was. Ethan's life was a short concerto.

There was one other thing I decided to do. I turned away from the mirror and went out into the living room. Mom was in the kitchen. "I'm going for a walk," I called and opened the door.

The October sun was warm, but not too hot. I headed toward the camp gate. At Liz's house I stopped and knocked on the door.

Liz had on jeans and a pink shirt. She sort of sucked in her breath when she saw me. "I have to go on an errand," I said. "Will you walk with me?"

"Where are you going?" she asked.

"Down to the McGuires'," I told her. "I have to ask for a puppy."

"I'll go with you," she said.

I knew she would.

The little ball of black fur Liz and I carried home that day is a big dog now, almost three years old. Tonight I will wear a blue cap and gown and march with the others into our auditorium.

I will not mention Motie Ann or Ethan by name in

my graduation speech, but I will urge my classmates to work for their dreams, to listen for life's music, and to appreciate people who are different.

Liz will be beside me tonight. When I take my seat after my speech, I know she will smile and squeeze my arm. I'll turn to see her face. Liz is a mirror, reflecting so much of me, and Ethan will be there between us always, once a division, now a bond.